Praise for *American Estrangement*

"[Saïd] Sayrafiezadeh captures one of the most essential feelings of the modern-day United States, apathy, and holds us to that feeling. The result is . . . [a] depiction of deterioration and uncertainty in a changing nation."
—Malavika Praseed, *Chicago Review of Books*

"The consummate outsider, Sayrafiezadeh examines our nation's sins with a particularly clear eye, and his latest collection of short stories, *American Estrangement*, is no exception." —*Millions*

"*American Estrangement* is Saïd Sayrafiezadeh's . . . best book to date. . . . [T]here is a compelling combination of realism and allegory and some dystopian flourishes."
—Arin Keeble, *Times Literary Supplement*

"Lyrical, funny, smart, and heartbreaking."
—*Kirkus Reviews*, starred review

"[A] rich collection. . . . Sayrafiezadeh vividly captures his characters' misplaced optimism, which is what makes these stories so moving." —*Publishers Weekly*

"Sayrafiezadeh, entertaining and political without being heavy-handed, is a force to be reckoned with." —*Booklist*

AMERICAN ESTRANGEMENT

AMERICAN ESTRANGEMENT

stories

SAÏD SAYRAFIEZADEH

W. W. NORTON & COMPANY
Celebrating a Century of Independent Publishing

Copyright © 2021 by Saïd Sayrafiezadeh
All rights reserved
Printed in the United States of America
First published as a Norton paperback 2023

"Audition" and "Last Meal at Whole Foods" originally appeared in *The New Yorker*. "Audition" also appeared in *Best American Stories 2019*. "Metaphor of the Falling Cat" originally appeared in *The Paris Review*.

For information about permission to reproduce selections from this book, write to Permissions, W. W. Norton & Company, Inc., 500 Fifth Avenue, New York, NY 10110

For information about special discounts for bulk purchases, please contact W. W. Norton Special Sales at specialsales@wwnorton.com or 800-233-4830

Manufacturing by LSC Communications, Harrisonburg
Production manager: Lauren Abbate

Library of Congress Cataloging-in-Publication Data

Names: Sayrafiezadeh, Saïd, author.
Title: American estrangement : stories / Saïd Sayrafiezadeh.
Description: First edition. | New York : W. W. Norton & Company, 2021.
Identifiers: LCCN 2020053360 | ISBN 9780393541236 (hardcover) |
ISBN 9780393541243 (epub)
Subjects: LCGFT: Short stories.
Classification: LCC PS3619.A998 A84 2021 | DDC 813/.6—dc23
LC record available at https://lccn.loc.gov/2020053360

ISBN 978-1-324-05048-3 pbk.

W. W. Norton & Company, Inc., 500 Fifth Avenue, New York, N.Y. 10110
www.wwnorton.com

W. W. Norton & Company Ltd., 15 Carlisle Street, London W1D 3BS

1 2 3 4 5 6 7 8 9 0

In memory of my mother, Martha Harris née Finkelstein,
who knew estrangement

CONTENTS

AUDITION

The first time I smoked crack cocaine was the spring I worked construction for my father on his new subdivision in Moonlight Heights. My original plan had been to go to college, specifically for the arts, specifically for acting, where I'd envisioned strolling shoeless around campus with a notepad, jotting down details about the people I observed so that I would later be able to replicate the human condition on-screen with nuance and veracity. Instead, I was unmatriculated and nineteen, working six days a week, making eight dollars an hour, no more or less than what the other general laborers were being paid, and which is what passed, at least for my self-made father, as fairness. Occasionally I would be cast in a community theater production of Neil Simon or *The Mystery of Edwin Drood*, popular but uncomplicated fare, which we would rehearse for a month before performing in front of an audience of fifteen. "You have to pay your dues," the older actors would tell me, sensing, I suppose, my disappointment and impatience. "How long is that going to take?" I'd ask them, as if they spoke from high atop the pinnacle of show business. In lieu of an answer, they offered a tautology. "It takes as long as it takes," they'd say.

It was spring, it was rainy, it was the early nineties, meaning that *Seinfeld* was all the rage, and so was Michael Jordan, and so was crack cocaine, the latter of which, at this point, I had no firsthand knowledge. As for Jerry Seinfeld and Michael Jordan, I knew them well. Each evening, having spent my day carrying sixty-pound drywall across damp pavement and up bannisterless staircases in one of the state-of-the-art family residences being pre-wired for the Internet—whatever that was—in a cul-de-sac eventually to be named Placid Village Circle, I would drive to my apartment and watch one or the other, Seinfeld or Jordan, since one or the other always happened to be on. They were famous, they were artists, they were exalted. I watched them and dreamed of my own fame and art and exalt. The more I dreamed, the more vivid the dream seemed to be, until it was no longer some faint dot situated on an improbable time line but, rather, my *destiny*. And all I needed to turn this destiny into reality was to make it out of my midsized city—not worth specifying—and move to L.A., where, of course, an actor needed to be if he was to have any chance at that thing called success. But, from my perspective of a thousand miles, L.A. appeared immense, incensed, inscrutable, impenetrable, and every time I thought I had enough resolve to uproot myself and rent a U-Haul I would quickly retreat into the soft, downy repetitiveness of my hometown, with its low stakes, high livability, and steady paycheck from my father.

The general laborers came and went that spring, working for a few weeks and then quitting without notice, eight dollars apparently not being enough to compensate even the most unskilled. No matter. For every man who quit, there were five more waiting in line to take his place, eight dollars apparently being enough to fill any vacancy. I was responsible for showing the new recruits around on their first day, which took about twenty minutes and got me out of carrying drywall. Here's the porta-potty. Here's the foreman's office. Here's the paper to sign. They wanted to know what the job was like. They wanted to know if there were health benefits. They spoke quietly and conspiratorially, as if what they asked might be perceived as treasonous. They wanted to know if they might have the opportunity to learn some plumbing or carpentry. "You'll have to talk to the boss about that," I'd tell them, but the answer was no. What they should have been asking me was if there was a union.

No one knew that I was the boss's son. About once a week my dad would show up in his powder-blue Mercedes and walk around inspecting the progress, displeased and concerned, finding everything urgent and subpar, showing neither love nor special dispensation toward me, nor did I show any toward him. This seemed to come easily to the two of us. I was just another workingman in wet overalls and he was just another big shot in a three-piece suit and a safety vest. The roles we played were generic, superficial, and true. Later, he'd tell me, "I'm doing this for you, not for me." What "this" was, was not entirely clear. "One day all of this will be yours," he'd say. "This" was three sub-divisions and a ten-story office building downtown. "This" was the powder-blue Mercedes. According to my father, he wanted me to learn the meaning of hard work up close and personal so that I would know what life was really like, but also because he wanted me to experience what he had gone through growing up on the outskirts of town with six siblings, odd jobs, and no help from the government. In short, I was living a version of his life, albeit in reverse.

From time to time, I would be paired up with a guy named Duncan Dioguardi, who was my age but looked ten years older, and who liked to order me around—put this here, put that there. He enjoyed the power, while I enjoyed the cold comfort of knowing that I could burst his bubble by telling him who my dad was, but a good actor never breaks character. Clearly, I was a novice and not very good at hard work, as Duncan and my father had already surmised. I got winded fast. I got apathetic fast. I cut corners when I could. I waited for opportunities to go to the porta-potty. I waited for opportunities to smoke cigarettes. The cigarettes got me winded faster. "You need to get into shape," Duncan would tell me. "Why don't you use your next paycheck to buy yourself a ThighMaster?" This was a joke for him. He would walk around in short-sleeved shirts, impervious to the chill, a tattoo of a snake coiling around his bicep and crawling up toward his neck, en route to devour his face, a dramatic and striking image if ever there was one, doubly so against his pale skin, slick with drizzle. In the meantime, I slouched beneath drywall, imagining L.A. in the spring, waiting for lunchtime, quite proficient at not being the boss's son, and all the while reassuring myself that one day in the future I would be performing some version of this role with nuance and veracity, out of shape or not. "What did you draw from to create the character?" the critics would ask me. "Why, from real life," I would say.

When lunchtime arrived, I'd sit around with the other general laborers, thirty of us on upturned crates in an unfinished living room with a spring breeze blowing through the glassless windows, eating roast-beef sandwiches and talking about money problems, home problems, work problems. My problems were not their problems, but I wished they were. Their problems were immediate, distinct, and resolvable; mine were long-term, existential, and impossible. When I spoke, I tried to approximate the speech patterns of my coworkers—the softened consonants and the dropped articles—lest I reveal myself as the outsider that I was. No hard k's, x's, or f's. The irony was that my father's specified plan of self-improvement for me dovetailed with my own: experience real life up close and personal.

The other general laborers knew one another from high school or the neighborhood or the previous work site, which had paid ten dollars an hour. They hoped that the subdivision wouldn't be finished until fall, maybe even winter. They didn't mind working forever. They were still counting on a chance to learn a trade—but half of them would be gone in two weeks. As for me, I'd grown up in Timpani Hills, where none of these men would have had any reason to visit unless they'd come to do some roofing. I'd gone to the best schools and had the cushiest upbringing, including a pool in the backyard and weekend acting classes, where my dad would watch me perform on parents' night, misty and proud in the front row, his boorishness temporarily abated, supportive of his son's passion and talent until he realized that his son was intending to pursue acting as something more than a hobby. Now all that history was inconsequential, pulsed inside the blender of collective toil. No one would have been able to tell me apart from any of the other general laborers I sat with on my lunch break, smoking cigarettes amid exposed crossbeams. Just as no one would have been able to tell that I was the boss's son. To the latecomer entering the theater, I was indistinguishable from the whole.

Just as no one would have been able to tell that I didn't really want to give Duncan Dioguardi a lift to his house after work, but his car had broken down—yet one more item to be added to the list of immediate problems. What I wanted to say was, "Why don't you ride home on a Thigh-Master?" But what I actually said was, "Sure, jump in!" I could hear the sprightliness in my voice, all false. It was Saturday. It was four o'clock. The foreman was letting us off early because the drywall hadn't been delivered on time. The new recruits wondered if they would still be paid for a full day. Theirs was an argument that made sense only on paper. "Go enjoy the weather," the foreman said, as if he were bestowing the good weather upon us. Indeed, the sun was high and there was no rain. When the breeze blew, it blew with promise. I should have been savoring the first official nice day of spring; instead, I was driving an hour out of my way down Route 15. The traffic was slow going. We stopped and started. We stopped again. Duncan Dioguardi apologized for the traffic. Inside the car he was surprisingly thoughtful and courteous. He had his seat belt on and his hands were folded in his lap. "Setting is everything," my dear old acting teacher had once told me, and then we had done exercises to illustrate this concept: forest, beach, prison cell.

"I don't mind traffic," I told Duncan. I was being courteous, too. I softened my consonants. I dropped my articles. Through the windshield, our midsized city crawled past at a midsized pace. Midsized highways with midsized cars. Midsized citizens with their midsized lives.

We talked about work and then we talked about ourselves. Away from the subdivision, it was clear that we had little in common. He told me that he'd been doing manual labor since he was fifteen, beginning with cleaning bricks at a demolition site on the north side of the city. I was taking weekend acting classes at fifteen. "A nickel a brick," Duncan told me. "You do the math." I wasn't sure what math there was to do. Duncan was the one who should have been taking acting classes, not me, receiving instruction on how to transform his supply of hard-earned material into that thing called art. He'd already lived twice the life that I'd lived, while having none of my advantages. He was what my father had been before my father hit it big. But Duncan Dioguardi was most likely never going to hit it big. His trajectory seemed already established. If I wasn't careful, *my* trajectory would soon be established. The tattoo of the snake heading up to Duncan's face was not an affect but as apt a metaphor as any of what the past had been like for him, and what the future held. He needed no affect. *I* was the one who needed an affect. "Don't ever get a tattoo," my acting teacher had told me. "A performer must always remain a blank slate." So here I was, playing the role of general laborer, with flawless skin and stuck in traffic.

It was four-thirty. If I was lucky, I'd be home by six. Maybe I would take a nap, assuage my fatigue and apathy, wake up fresh, and do something productive, like read a script and enlighten myself. Sometimes I would lie in the bathtub and read aloud from my stack of current and classic screenplays, playing every single character, men, women, and children. Even the stage directions were a character: *Fade in. Int. bathtub—night. Fade out.* Everything was deserving of voice. Meanwhile, Duncan Dioguardi and I lit cigarettes, one after the other, inhaling first- and secondhand smoke. We fiddled with the radio. Tupac came on. Tupac was all the rage. We nodded our heads to Tupac. Apropos of Tupac, I told Duncan about how I was planning to move to L.A. I said it casually, as if this plan were already in the works rather than a doubtful dot on an undrawn time line, and I was unexpectedly filled with a brief but heartening sense that, merely by my vocalizing that something would happen, something would actually happen—as per pop psychology. Duncan told me that he had lived in L.A., between starting high school and dropping out of high school. What else had Duncan done by the age of nineteen? Where else had Duncan lived? He was so far ahead of me in the category of life that I would have been unable to catch up even if I began living *now*. "What was L.A. like?" I asked him. I could hear my counterfeit casualness being usurped by genuine yearning. "It was magical," Duncan said. He got quiet. He contributed no follow-up details. He stared out the windshield. "See this traffic?" he said. I saw this traffic. "This isn't L.A. traffic," he said. I pictured L.A. traffic on a Saturday at four-thirty, sun high, never rain, bumper-to-bumper, all of it magical.

Suddenly I was telling Duncan Dioguardi about my innermost desires, speaking confessionally, spilling my guts, spelling out exactly how I was going to become an actor, how I was going to rent a U-Haul, not give the boss any notice, fuck the boss, drive a thousand miles in a day, arrive in L.A., find an agent, find a place to live, start auditioning for film and television, maybe even *Seinfeld*. "Keep an eye out for me on *Seinfeld*," I said. If you say it, it will happen. Somewhere along the way, I had stopped dropping articles and softening consonants, because it was too difficult a ruse to maintain while also trying to be authentic. I told Duncan about having performed in *The Mystery of Edwin Drood*, twice, at the rec center, one fall and the following fall. I'd had only a small part but I'd got some laughs. I didn't tell him that there'd been fifteen people in the audience. Perhaps he'd heard of the production? There had been a four-star review in the *Tribune*. No, he hadn't heard of it.

"You can do better than that bullshit," he said.

———

It was five o'clock. We were moving fast now. The traffic was gone. So were my cigarettes. We were inspiring each other with our uplifting stories of promise and potential. Duncan was telling me about his own plans for the future, which mainly involved having realized that he'd wasted the previous year, and the year before that. He was determined to make up for it. He knew precisely what needed to be done. He spoke generally. In response, I spoke generally, too, providing platitudes where applicable. "You can do whatever you set your mind to," I said. "It's mind over matter," he said. "That's right!" I said. "That's right!" he said. We were in agreement, and yet I had the peculiar feeling that we were referring to different things.

He was telling me where to turn. Turn here. Turn there. Left. Right. Right. I was entering territory with which I was unfamiliar, because I'd grown up cushy. We drove beneath an overpass that led into a down-and-out neighborhood of weather-beaten, two-story, red-brick homes, a hundred of them in a row, every one identical, just as the houses in my father's subdivision were identical, but at the other end of the economic spectrum. This was a neighborhood of odd jobs and no help, where people shopped for dinner at the convenience store. "I trust them as far as I can throw them," Duncan said, referring to I know not what. This was outsized struggle in a midsized city. Turn. Turn. Turn. The Spice Girls came on. The Spice Girls were all the rage. Apropos of the Spice Girls, Duncan was asking me if I wanted to party tonight. He was asking as if the thought had just occurred to him. It was Saturday, after all. It was five-thirty. It would be a shame to let these windfall spring hours go to waste. It would be a shame to go home as I always did, lie in the bathtub, have another night of living life through the soggy pages of screenplays, getting closer to twenty years old, my time line unraveling like a ball of yarn. I somehow knew that the word "party" in this context meant one thing: getting high. What I really wanted was to stop at a convenience store and get more cigarettes. "Don't waste your money," Duncan said. He could buy me more cigarettes, no problem. He pointed to one of the identical buildings. If I gave him ten dollars he could get me a carton of cigarettes at half price. If I chipped in thirty dollars he could get the two of us cigarettes *plus*. "Do you want cigarettes *plus*?" Duncan asked. "Do you want to party?" He was speaking now entirely in the language of euphemisms, and I was fluent.

"Yes," I said. "I want to party."

It was six o'clock and we were in the basement of Duncan Dioguardi's house. Or, more to the point, we were in the basement of his *mother's* house, where he was staying until his security deposit cleared. "Banks," he said, generally. His mother wasn't home, but she kept a nice house, much nicer on the inside than it appeared on the outside, with hardwood floors and crown molding, and I thought about how these were the kinds of detail that would have eluded a person who had merely driven through the neighborhood without bothering to stop, like the passenger on a cruise ship who thinks he knows the island from the port. Duncan's basement was more bedroom than basement, with Mom's touches, sheets tucked in, cozy and comfortable, except for a boiler in the corner that was making clicking sounds. Stacked up in a pile were some carpentry manuals for beginners, yellow books with hammers on the covers. "I dabble with those sometimes," he said. Then he added, "But they won't give a guy like me a chance." I wasn't sure if "whatever you set your mind to" would apply in this instance.

On his dresser was a Magnavox TV, twenty-five-inch, with a built-in VCR, presumably left on all day, tuned to ESPN, where the announcers were oohing and aahing over, who else, Michael Jordan, who was doing, what else, winning. He glided down the court. He floated through the air. He elbowed his defender in the chest. Everything he did had style, even his mistakes. He was the perfect blend of beauty and power, of grace and aggression. No one would have dared tell Michael Jordan, "It takes as long as it takes."

My carton of cigarettes was in my lap, cradled lovingly, half price, as promised, already torn open by me, cigarette smoke going straight up into my face, and in Duncan's palm was the adventure I had come here for, two small white cubes—yellowish, really, crumbs, really—bought at full price. "This is what you get for twenty dollars apiece," he said. "You do the math." Had I been the latecomer to this play, I would have thought that these two small cubes had been chipped off the edge of some drywall, so insignificant did they look. If Duncan had accidentally dropped them on the floor, they would have been lost forever in the grain of the hardwood. But Duncan, handling them with such care and attention, as if he were a doctor operating over a nightstand, demonstrating speed and precision, using one of Mom's table knives to gently break the two white chips into even smaller white chips, would never let them drop on the floor. This was the stuff of theater, basement theater, the six o'clock show, and I had a front-row seat to the action, from which I was able to watch what happens when the actor does not have the right props with him, because this actor is "not a pro, and not intending on becoming a pro." What Duncan was, though, was ingenious, withdrawing a roll of aluminum foil from beneath his bed, no doubt procured from Mom's cupboard, and a box of Chore Boy, also from beneath his bed, with little Chore Boy wearing a backward baseball cap, a big grin on his face, because life is nothing if not delightful, especially when one is cleaning. He could have been a character from a fairy tale, Chore Boy, innocent and archetypal, his stumpy arm beckoning the consumer toward some enchanted land. Soon a perfect aluminum-foil pipe emerged from Duncan Dioguardi, glinting silver in the Magnavox light, reminding me of the way some family restaurants will wrap your leftovers in aluminum foil in the shape of a swan. But into this particular swan's mouth disappeared a piece of the Chore Boy, followed by one small chip off the drywall, and then Duncan Dioguardi ran his lighter back and forth, orange flame on silver neck, and from the swan's tail he sucked ever so gently, cheeks pulling, pulling, until, like magic, he tilted his head back and out of his mouth emerged a perfect puff of white smoke.

He considered for a moment, eyes closed, then eyes opened, gauging, I suppose, the ratio of crack cocaine to baking powder, and then he offered an appraisal. "Not bad," he said. He looked at me. Was it my turn now?

No, not yet my turn. First we must watch Michael Jordan, because the aluminum-foil pipe needed time to cool down, a necessary and dramatic interlude, the basement boiler ticking off the minutes. It was almost the end of the basketball game, and beads of sweat dripped elegantly down Jordan's shaved head as he huddled with coaches and teammates, half listening to advice that had long ago ceased applying to him. He showed no signs of trepidation or anxiety about the fate of the game. He already *knew* the fate of the game. As for the advice that Duncan Dioguardi was now offering me, I listened carefully. This is how you hold the pipe. This is how you inhale the smoke. "This isn't

a cigarette," he said. "You don't suck it into your lungs."
He was patient, the way a good coach should be. Then he
clicked the lighter and I was pulling as he had pulled, not
too hard, not too soft, just right. I had expected the foil on
my lips to taste like something, but it tasted like nothing.
I had expected the smoke to smell like something, but it
smelled like nothing. I had expected the high to alter me
in some profound and mystifying way, but the effect was
underwhelming and anticlimactic. Mostly, I felt clear-eyed
and levelheaded, disappointingly so. "Not bad," I said anyway. The only thing that was unexpected was the sudden
sense of fondness that I had for Duncan Dioguardi, good
coach that he was, and, dare I say, good friend. Sure, I barely
knew him; sure, we had had different upbringings; but we
had shared something on that ride down Route 15, and
we were sharing something now, within his home, which
he had welcomed me into, and in this way, yes, I could
consider him a friend. The passenger who had remained
only in the port, browsing the trinket shops, delighting in
duty-free, would never have known this subtle but essential
detail. Just as he would never have known that there was
indeed a distinct smell hovering in the room, of the Chore
Boy being cooked alive, not dissimilar to the odor when the
plumbers had come through the subdivision, soldering the
water lines, the new recruits watching them with envy and
admiration.

That spring, my dear old acting teacher came to my rescue by way of a phone call, out of the blue, asking if I might be available to audition for a play that he was directing at the Apple Tree Theatre. "So wonderful to hear your voice again," he said. He said that he had always remembered me fondly from those Sunday classes years earlier—Intro to Acting I, followed by Intro to Acting II—where he would instruct a dozen teenagers in the world of make-believe. We played games, we played inanimate objects, we played adults. "There are rules even for make-believe," he would tell us. Everything he said had the ring of truth and revelation. He had the empathy and kindness of the elderly. If there had been an Intro III and IV, I would have taken those, too, all the way up to C. I was always forlorn when my dad arrived to pick me up in his powder-blue Mercedes, the engine kept running. On a few occasions, my teacher had taken him aside and told him that his son had a future in theater. "That's good to know," my father had said, but the future he was envisioning was real estate.

Now my teacher was calling to say that he had never forgotten me, that I had made a strong impression on him, even at the age of fifteen, and that he thought I would be perfect for the role he had in mind. The way he spoke made it sound as if he had already come to a decision and reading for the role was only a technicality. Still, I knew enough to know that nothing was ever guaranteed, that auditioning was only one step toward being cast, that a play was only one step toward a movie, and a movie was only one step toward fame. But that my teacher had sought me out after all these years was a sign that I was truly talented, that the hope I had been harboring was not false, and that I was living a life where the unexpected could indeed occur.

When I showed up for the audition a week later, I was disheartened to see that it was far from a foregone conclusion. I was one of twenty young men who had apparently all been students of my acting teacher, and all of whom he had apparently remembered fondly. We were perfect replicas of one another, dressed in khakis, hair blow-dried, walking around doing the same vocal warm-ups that we had been taught: *B-B-B-B, T-T-T-T*—no softened consonants here. In our hands we held headshots of our giant faces, lit to make us appear older, wiser, and better-looking than we actually were, and on the back were our résumés, numbering ten or fewer credentials, twice for *The Mystery of Edwin Drood*. In thirty years, the list of credentials would be longer and our headshots would be younger.

Things were running behind. The auditions were supposed to have started at ten o'clock, first come, first served, but it was noon and they'd made it only through twelve hopefuls. I was No. 19 on the list. I was anxious. I was hungry. I was taking time off from work. "A dentist's appointment," I'd told the foreman. "Do that on your own time," he'd said. Instead of eating food, I smoked cigarettes, standing in the doorway, six feet from a sign that said NO SMOKING, exhaling out into the spring air, alongside my fellow actors who looked like me. We bantered, we joked, we lit one another's cigarettes, we pretended we were not consumed with insecurity and competitiveness. To help pass the time we talked about classical and postmodern theater. If I had gone to college, I might have known what I was talking about. The walls around us were adorned with posters of plays past, announcing four-week runs to nowhere. Every so often the big brown door of the theater, with its single round pane of glass, something like a porthole, would swing open, off-loading the previous aspirant, a carbon copy of myself, whose face conveyed, in equal parts, relief, defeat, and premature delusions of being cast.

When it was finally my turn, I was surprised to see that my acting teacher, whom I had remembered at best as middle-aged, and at most as old, was probably only in his early thirties. He had seemed tall back then, too, but now he was short and I was tall. He was standing in the middle of a row of seats, with stacks of scripts beside him, and when I handed him my headshot he looked at me without the faintest recognition, but then when it suddenly became clear to him who I was and how much I'd changed in the intervening years he stepped forward and embraced me. I felt his empathy and kindness draped around my shoulders, expressed without reservation, and if the embrace had continued much longer I might have cried. He wanted to know how I'd been, and what I'd been doing, but since the auditions were running behind there was no time to catch up.

What was being decided here and now was whether I would be cast in a central role as a character who would be onstage for all three acts but had zero lines. I could not tell if this was a step backward or forward for my career. If I had to pick one, I would have picked backward. According to my teacher, it was forward. "He holds the play together," he said. To this end, he needed to see how I "move through space," since moving through space would be the only thing I would be doing. So I took my place onstage, apprehensive beneath a single blinding spotlight, and waited for his direction, which was, simply, "Show me the color red."

This was not something I had been anticipating. I had been anticipating, for example, being asked to mime pouring a glass of water, something I remember being quite good at. Without warning, we had entered the realm of symbolism and abstraction. We had entered game-playing and fun. But all I could think of was the tremendous predicament of being asked to embody a *concept*. Was a color even a concept? If I had been fifteen still, I would have done what he asked, happily, without thinking twice. I would have done every color. "Here's fuchsia!" "Here's cadmium yellow!" There would have been joy in exploration. Now my brain felt calcified and literal, the effects of aging. I could think only of making a semi-bold choice, like lying on my back and moving interpretatively. But lying on my back would obscure me from my teacher's vision. "If the audience can't see you," he would sometimes say, "then who are you doing this for?" I lay down anyway, the hard stage pressing against me, dust getting all over my khakis. The foreman would say to me later, "You got dirty from going to the dentist?" For lack of any other idea, I channeled the character of the foreman, and then I channeled the drywall, which was not a character, and I thought about smoking a cigarette, because in my world of make-believe the color red smokes cigarettes, which was what I did, lying on my back, eyes closed, moving conceptually, this way and that, blowing smoke into the yellow spotlight of blindness, and when I stood up and dusted myself off I had, most wondrously, been given the role.

The second time I smoked crack cocaine was the spring I worked construction for my father on his new subdivision in Moonlight Heights. By this point, the electricians had finished pre-wiring for the Internet, whatever that was, the floors had been poured, the windows had been installed, and the general laborers had come and gone, eight dollars an hour not being enough. I would show the new recruits around, bathroom, foreman, paper to sign, and then I would go carry drywall in the sunshine. I was aware that I had been waiting for Duncan Dioguardi to invite me to party again, but no invitation had been forthcoming, and to broach it myself seemed as though it would traverse an essential but unstated boundary.

This time it was a Tuesday evening, after our shift, around six o'clock. Duncan's car had broken down again. "Sure," I said, "jump in." I could hear the sprightliness in my voice, now authentic. The traffic was just as bad as ever and we crawled forward with our windows rolled down, the spring breeze blowing in, the cigarette smoke blowing out, dusk all around us. "I'm sorry about the traffic," Duncan said, as he had said before. "I don't mind," I said. We talked about the subdivision for a while, and then we were quiet, mulling over I know not what, and then I broke the silence with the fantastic news that I'd been cast in a play, and that the way I saw things it was only a matter of time before I would be renting the U-Haul and making my move.

Duncan was happy for me. He shook my hand. He slapped me on the back. "Whatever you set your mind to," he said. I told him that I'd get him a free ticket for opening night. He told me, "I'll be able to tell people I knew you *when*." I was not used to such expansiveness. I could feel myself blushing. "Not many lines," I told him. Obviously, the truth was that there were *no* lines. But I thought it was important to at least try to keep things in some perspective. Humility first, fame second.

"Lines don't matter," Duncan said. Success was what mattered, and success called for celebration.

"Aw," I said, "I sure appreciate that." But it was a work night, after all.

No, it wasn't. It wasn't even seven o'clock. It would be a shame to let such good news go to waste. "Let's celebrate," Duncan Dioguardi said.

I knew that, in this context, "celebrate" was another word for "party," which was, of course, itself another word.

The traffic was gone and I was driving fast. If I had had an ability to observe myself, I might have questioned why I needed to get where I was going in such a hurry. Under the overpass I went, fifteen miles above the speed limit. Turn, turn, turn. Duncan Dioguardi didn't need to tell me where to turn. He wanted to know if I had forty dollars to chip in. For forty dollars I'd have to stop at the ATM. The ATM was in the convenience store, where people were shopping for dinner. At the ATM, I noted with satisfaction that my savings were considerable—eight dollars an hour adds up.

His mother was home when we got there. "Meet my friend," Duncan Dioguardi said. The word "friend" was not a euphemism. His mother was sitting in the living room watching *Seinfeld*. She said, "You're welcome here anytime." She was being warm. She was being hospitable. She was laughing at what was happening on TV, and a few moments later Duncan and I were in the basement, also laughing at what was happening on TV. Jerry was saying something logical, and George was frustrated, and Elaine was rolling her eyes, and here came Kramer bursting through the front door. When Duncan opened his hand, I imagined for a moment that, instead of the insignificant chips off the drywall, he was holding a palmful of giant chunks, the size of golf balls, one pound each.

"You do the math," Duncan said.

Beneath his bed was the Chore Boy, but its symbolism had gone the way of the euphemism. Now when we smoked, we used, of all things, a broken car antenna, which, according to Duncan, he had found lying on the sidewalk. This was a neighborhood where car antennas lay on the sidewalk. The smoke came out of Duncan's mouth in the same white puff that lingered in the air of the basement theater. "Not bad," he said, again. And when it was my turn I also said, "Not bad," but I meant it this time. I was the passenger on the cruise ship who has become acquainted with the island. The same warm feeling of friendship for Duncan engulfed me, followed by an unexpected but welcome sense of optimism concerning my prospects—extraordinarily promising they were, weren't they, beginning with those three acts I was going to have onstage and heading toward a career. It was eight o'clock. Another episode of *Seinfeld* was just getting under way, the back-to-back shows courtesy of NBC, the interweaving story lines being established in that first minute: someone determined, someone displeased, the fatal flaw introduced, followed, thirty minutes later, by the abrupt resolution, and all of it funny, until all of it suddenly was *not* funny.

Suddenly I was in possession of that thing called clarity. I was watching the most vapid show in the history of television—it had always been vapid and we, the viewers, had always been duped. I could see straight through it now—solipsistic, narcissistic, false reality, easy tropes, barely amusing. The clarity that I *thought* I'd had moments earlier had not been clarity at all but, rather, its opposite, delusion, which was now being usurped by an all-encompassing awareness, horrible and heavy, through which I understood at once that I was not talented, had never been talented, that my life as a general laborer was proof of this lack of talent, and that being cast in a role with zero lines was not a step toward fame but a step into obscurity in a midsized city. Who but a fool agrees to move through space for three acts without saying a word?

The car antenna was coming back my way. It was nine o'clock. I had entered a strange dimension of time—it was progressing both slowly and quickly, as marked by the ticking of that basement boiler. Nine was early for night. It would be night for many more hours to come. I was nineteen. Nineteen was young. I would be young for many more years to come. What exactly had I been so troubled by a few minutes before? Light and airy clarity descended upon me. Ah, *this* was clarity, and the other, delusion. I had reversed things, silly, overstated them, compounded them, turned delight into cynicism. I was going to be onstage for three acts, moving through space, another credential to have on my résumé when I arrived in L.A. It was ten o'clock. Was ten o'clock early for night? Was night moving slowly or fast? Was Jerry funny or stupid? We were driving back to the ATM now. I knew I was traversing some essential but unstated boundary, but I traversed it anyway. I wondered if Duncan Dioguardi had ever had a broken-down car or if he had smoked the car, its antenna being the last piece remaining. I wondered if he'd smoked L.A. I wondered if he'd one day smoke his Magnavox TV. This is the last time I'm doing this, I said to myself, even as I knew that saying so implied its inverse. At the ATM, I took out another forty dollars. I noted my balance. My savings account was still large. It was midnight. Midnight was still young.

SCENIC ROUTE

t's around six months or so after society has begun changing, mainly for the worse, when Lizzy and I decide to take that trip we've been talking about for so long, and which, only in hindsight, is probably our biggest mistake, i.e., not knowing what we're getting ourselves into. But she'll be turning forty soon, and I've already turned forty, and if we don't do it now, we'll never do it and instead we'll just talk about doing it. "Now or never," she says, and I'm sure she's right, because the most I've seen of the world has been this or that suburb. Besides, Lizzy says, no one can predict in what other ways society might begin changing—for the

worse—and I'm sure she's right about this, too, even though
I suspect she's not just referring to society, but to *us*, meaning her and me. In any case, I mail in the applications for
our travel documents, everything signed in triplicate and
notarized, and they're approved without incident, and a few
weeks after that we take two flights and one three-hour
layover, also without incident, arriving in Maine, which is
where our trip is officially beginning, at the Hertz rental car
agency, at the top, in Maine, where you can't go any higher
these days without having better paperwork, and our plan
is to take the long way down, back roads and such, because
that's the point, after all: to take the long way down before
it's too late.

Nor is there any indication of trouble from the rental
car agent, who's all smiles and New England goodness,
eighteen years old and working his summer job. "Where
you folks from?" he wants to know. He calls us "folks."
He thinks we're married but we're not. Later, Lizzy will
say, "Why does he need to know where we're from?" But
she's only being paranoid and he's only being nice. He's
surrounded by Hertz logos and fluorescent lights, telling us
that there just so happens to be a Cadillac Escalade in the
parking lot if we're interested, "just so happens," five-door,
full speed, which he can get for us at a great deal. He does a
good job pretending as if he's as surprised as anyone by how
great and unexpected a deal this is, but no doubt he's reading off a script from somewhere inside his head, his eyes

moving back and forth across the page, watermarked with his commission. "We were hoping for something cheap and simple," I tell him, by which I mean two doors and good mileage. Lizzy has other ideas. "Oh, let's live a little!" she says, never mind that we're trying to be budget-conscious on a vacation that hasn't even started. She's implying, publicly, that I alone stand as the obstacle to delight and merriment, and therefore joy and happiness. The eighteen-year-old can tell he's making progress with at least one of the folks, and so he goes ahead and gives us the hard sell on the upgrade, and I must admit that the Cadillac Escalade does sound awfully good, what with the tinted sunroof, the leather steering wheel, the dual DVD players "for the kids," which we don't have. The idea of luxury, even rented luxury, is appealing to me, as I know it must be for Lizzy, having grown up, as she did, *without.* "Sure, why not," I say, "let's live a little!" And Lizzy drapes her arms around me, asking, "Do you mean it?" as if the choice were only ever mine. I make a big show of removing the joint credit card from my wallet. Beneath the fluorescent light the card appears burnished and indestructible, despite an outsized monthly balance about which, as with many things, Lizzy and I have grown accustomed to deferring. All that matters now, though, is that the card is swiped through without complication, granting us access to that coveted crimson key fob that matches the coveted crimson Cadillac Escalade that just so happens to be in the parking lot. "Where you folks headed?" the agent wants to know. This is the last line of the script and he doesn't really care where we're headed. But it doesn't matter, because we don't really know.

Two hours later, Lizzy and I are reclining in rented luxury on credit, the daylight streaming velvet through the tinted sunroof, having made it as far as some town called Hamlin, population few. We see the sign and then the sign is gone. Lizzy's doing forty miles an hour, mostly she's doing thirty, at this rate it'll take us a week to make it through Maine, but this is the remedy that she has proposed. "The scenic route," Lizzy says. "Slow driving," she says. Slow driving, slow living. She has her finger on the pulse of "what ails us"—she's referring to society and also the *collective* us. When she's not working her day job at low pay, she's a yoga instructor above a natural foods store, three nights a week and Sundays, immersed for an hour and fifteen minutes in the ancient science of remedying and restoring one body at a time. That she is now steering a Cadillac Escalade down a country road, guzzling gas at twentysomething a gallon, is a contradiction in lifestyle that we have agreed to accept without further inquiry. Together we stare out at the thera-peutic landscape, mesmerized by the stillness, by the emp-tiness, by the rolling hills, etc. When we hit a bump in the road, we don't feel a thing. We are sailing more than we are riding. "Undulating," Lizzy says. She's talking about

the hills. We have our luggage in the back, along with a
cooler of green tea and room enough for eight more people.
Outside the car it smells of fresh air, and inside it smells of
air freshener. If society has changed, we can't tell through
the window.

And yet there is something that is clearly ailing us. What
it is precisely, no one has been able to determine, not even
the couples' counselor whom we went to see, one hundred
dollars out-of-network, with Lizzy and me sitting side by
side on the couch trying to account for a lack of delight and
merriment in our lives. We blamed ourselves, we blamed
our parents, mainly we blamed each other. After a year of
no improvement or discovery in either direction, we were
told by the couples' counselor, "I'm willing to keep seeing you but I'm not sure what would be gained." Standing
on the sidewalk in the wake of our last session, Lizzy had
said, "The board-certified professional admits defeat." We
continued onward, the two of us in our mid-thirties, occasionally evading, but never fully outrunning, a general dis-
satisfaction that now seems sure to tag along beside us into
middle age. Perhaps we met at the wrong point in life, or in
the wrong manner, i.e., online, where she'd lied about her
age, and I'd lied about my height *and* my age. "You have
a pretty smile," I'd written her, as vanilla a way as any to
break the ice, but which still managed to be effective. For
our first date we'd gotten together by the gazebo in the
business district, where, yes, she was older than I antici-

pated, but beautiful all the same, statuesque actually, and her brown hair was lush, and her smile indeed pretty. She'd been dressed in a skirt and sensible shoes, long legs, nice butt, having come from what she would refer to only as her sellout day job. As for me, I was neither beautiful nor lush, and my hair was thinning on top, which I knew would be evident given that we were equal in height. "What I really want to do is to make the world a better place," she'd told me within the first few minutes. I wasn't exactly sure what she'd meant by this. "That's a great idea!" I'd said.

Then we'd strolled out of the business district and into the natural foods store, because if you really want to break the ice, you do it by taking a yoga class together. I'd never done yoga before, but I'd wanted to show her that I was up for anything, an easygoing guy, fun-loving, wearing droopy pants with a drawstring, perched on the edge of a rubber mat in a room smelling of body odor and brown rice, making me think how everything was so laughably cliché, including Lizzy herself, who was going by the stage name *Saraswati*, with bare feet, turquoise earrings, and temperate voice, cooing her students into positions that I quickly realized I could never achieve without risking injury. Class had scarcely begun and I had sweat dripping off the tip of my nose, trying to twist to my right, trying to touch my toes, trying to focus on the light within or something. Lizzy had come over and adjusted me. "Like this," she'd whispered. Her hands were on the small of my back, pressing softly, as if there might be hope for me after all. "Breathe," she'd said, but I was already breathing, panting really. I was under the false impression, perhaps brought on by mental and physical exhaustion, that she had never touched anyone the way she was touching me. Later, she'd say, "I could feel the sadness in your body." She was talking about me, but she was also talking about her.

I'm wrong: we make it through Maine in a day and a half, staying overnight in a town called Yarmouth, about an hour from the border, where we hope to book a room in one of those old-timey inns, the kind from bygone days, with board games in the pantry, yogurt in the morning, and small talk about small-town life. But there are no inns in the vicinity, or bed-and-breakfasts, or lodges for that matter, an example of where society is heading, or where it has already arrived—this according to Lizzy. There is, however, a Motel 6, one story in taupe, where the attendant at the front desk also wants to know where we're from and also has "a great deal" on a room with a king-sized bed and spectacular views, plus free Wi-Fi with password. He pretends as if he's surprised by how great a deal all of this is. Again I hand over our joint credit card, which he swipes through without incident, granting Lizzy and me the electronic key that will get us into our room, Room 112, in taupe, and which, from first impressions, seems to have been designed with traveling executives in mind, swivel chair, charging station, walls covered with framed and mass-produced watercolors of Small-Town Past, all nature and shoppes and no people. But who are we trying to kid, we love this Room 112, despite the assembly-line feel, in fact, we love it *because* of the assembly-line feel. Here there is Wi-Fi and cable TV. Here there is no draftiness or creakiness or an innkeeper poking around at night. Here there are hotel toiletries, brand names in small bottles, which we will collect as we travel, every one of them, stock up for years and always remember *where we were when*. It's nearly dusk and the "spectacular view" we had been promised is limited to thirty yards from our window, through which we can see a teardrop swimming pool with a plaque that reads in indemnifying block print SWIM AT YOUR OWN RISK. Just beyond the swimming pool is our Cadillac Escalade, waiting patiently for us in the empty parking lot, its hood gradually transforming beneath the setting sun from crimson to ruby red, then, a moment later, an even darker shade of that, which is blood-red. Lizzy and I lie on our backs on the king-sized mattress, awed by the expanse, our fingers intertwined as we look up at the popcorn ceiling in taupe, saying nothing. I have a feeling that this might be the time for Lizzy to have "the talk" with me, or *a* talk, the first in a series, hopefully civil, about what the future holds for us, her and me. She'll begin lightly, politely, speaking gently, a soft-shoe prelude about everything we have done together, lo these last years, and everything that we can still do together, hypothetically speaking, with the years that remain. After which, the conversation will segue from everything we have *done* to everything we have *not* done, items fixed and indisputable, and which includes marriage and children, as if I alone stand as the obstacle.

But, lying there on the king-sized bed, our fingers intertwined, Lizzy broaches nothing, and neither do I, something soporific and soothing having apparently been induced by those three hundred slow-going miles in the Cadillac Escalade.

It's the next morning at the border between Maine and New Hampshire where things take a turn for the worse. "Have your travel documents ready," reads the LED display, but there are no patrolmen anywhere around. I pull into the designated spot, marked by official and inscrutable arrows, directly behind one other car, which is also waiting for the border patrol, and has, presumably, been waiting for quite some time, because the engine is off and the passengers seem to be dozing in the front seat. It occurs to me how few cars we have seen in our travels thus far, moreover, how few *people*, and that there has been a pervasive sense of abandonment or desertion. But this, of course, is because we have chosen to take the back roads, and here now before us is a subcompact with two doors, more toy than car, the type I had almost considered renting from Hertz back when I was in the habit of avoiding delight and merriment, which feels so long ago, and which I can say with confidence, sitting as I am in my leather seat with my leather steering wheel, surrounded by wood trim and chrome accents, with climate control set to perfect, that I am thankful for having made such personal growth. Indeed, I could sit here all day, gazing at the view where Maine becomes New Hampshire, a scene reminiscent of those watercolors from the walls of the Motel 6, pastoral, prosaic, no sound, all nature, Lizzy and me insulated within our Cadillac Escalade, the glowing knobs of the dashboard blinking at us with essential information, as if we are inside a spaceship *orbiting* the land, rather than *of* it.

"How long are we supposed to wait?" Lizzy asks.

"Slow waiting," I say. I thought this would go over well, but it does not. Evidently she is now in a hurry. She leans across me and presses hard on the horn, harder than necessary, longer than necessary, pushing with both hands. The horn sounds more like detonation than horn, and it disrupts the New England serenity, startling the passengers in the subcompact who are sitting upright and getting presentable for the authorities. I have a good feeling that *this*, this inconsiderate behavior by Lizzy, this *act against nature*, is going to be our first fight of the trip, and before I can fully work out an opening salvo that will cut hard and deep, the doors of the subcompact swing open, and instead of two chumps emerging from the car, I'm discomfited to see that it's actually two border patrolmen, dressed in dark blue uniforms, the New Hampshire coat of arms on one shoulder, the official bird, whatever it is, on the other. They are strapping, these patrolmen, six feet tall, barely fitting into their shirts, full heads of hair, no need here to lie about height or age, striding toward our Cadillac Escalade with the mistaken impression that it was *I*, not Lizzy, who had sounded the horn.

They tap on our windows with their flashlights as if they were the ones to have pulled up behind me, rather than the other way around, their silver rifles strung across their shoulders, long enough to be a third leg, appearing burnished and indestructible in the sunshine.

"Let's see your travel documents," they say without preamble.

Here we are not "folks." Here there is no New England goodness. Here we are playing solely by the rules.

Happily, our documents are in the glove compartment, six weeks in the bureaucratic making and all in order, but when I reach over and pop the glove compartment open, out they tumble, falling windswept across the floor mat emblazoned with the Hertz logo.

"You can't read the LED display?" the patrolmen ask. They are annoyed that I am not prepared, despite how much time I have had to do so, and this, I am sure, will be seen as an indication of out-of-state disrespect.

"Yes, sir," I say, "I sure can read it!" I hear the emasculation coating my voice and I'm helpless to stop it. Later, Lizzy will pile on about the importance of maintaining dignity, especially in the presence of authority, especially in this day and age. "When our self-respect goes," she will say, quoting someone, "what then will we be left with?"

The patrolmen shine their flashlights inside the car, looking for I know not what, the flashlight diffused by the sunlight coming through the sunroof. They want to know who we are. They want to know who we are to *each other*. They want to know what's in the cooler in the back.

"Sixteen bottles of green tea," Lizzy tells them.

"How do you know the exact number?" they ask. They suspect they're on to something.

"Because I bought them," she says matter-of-factly, "and I've drunk them." She has a hard edge in her voice. She's giving as good as she's getting. She would never allow herself to be deprived of self-respect, even if it means we are made to sit here for hours by a vindictive, protocol-obsessed border patrol, who can, if they want, terminate our journey and send us back up into Maine.

But the patrolmen seem to accept Lizzy's answer at face value, and they move on to a long list of other inquiries, learned at the academy, such as where our trip began, what time did we leave, where do we intend to go. They're leaning in through the open windows of the Cadillac Escalade, their chests filling the frame, as if they're just chatting with us. I get the sense that they're more bored than annoyed, and that we are their chief diversion for the day, a routine border stop that they will draw out until their shift is over. They would probably rather be policemen than patrolmen, occupying, as they do, the lowest rung of law enforcement, their principle activity guarding the state perimeter in snow, rain, and heat. When they shoot to kill it's almost always from a distance, and only after having chased some poor fool for half a mile through the New England underbrush.

"It took you that long to come this far?" they ask. Again they suspect they're on to something.

"The scenic route!" I say.

They think I'm being literal. "Which route is that?" they say.

"The zigzag route," Lizzy says.

"Is that so?" They don't know what either one of us is talking about.

They ask what business we have had in Maine and what business we will have in New Hampshire.

"No business," I say, "just personal." Child cheerful.

"What's wrong with your own state?" they want to know.

I'm not sure if this is a question for which I am supposed to have an answer. "Nothing is wrong with it," I say.

"Is that so?" they say. Then they take the travel documents from me and disappear back into the subcompact, the car sinking beneath their weight, our precious paperwork out of sight, being manhandled by bored and frustrated law enforcement who dream of greater glory.

Lizzy is muttering to herself, saying goddamn this, goddamn that.

"They can see you muttering," I say.

"Let them see me," she says.

She's going to make this worse for us and then she's going to blame society.

"What gives them the right to ask us anything?" Lizzy asks. I want to tell her that, first and foremost, their guns give them the right.

When the border patrolmen return, I am sad to see that they have carelessly rolled up our travel documents and are holding them as if they are batons with which they plan to beat against the windshield of our Cadillac Escalade.

They say, "Are you sure you didn't come all this way just to stay?"

"No, sir," I say.

"We're asking the lady," they say.

"Why would I want to stay?" Lizzy says.

"Why would you want to leave?" they say.

I have the troubling awareness that the patrolmen might be flirting with Lizzy, and have in fact been flirting with her the entire time, unbeknownst to me, this being their chief diversion until their shift ends.

But suddenly, the game is over, if ever it was a game, and they are unfurling our rolled-up travel documents, already having been stamped with that most coveted phrase ENTRY

PERMITTED, below the raised seal of New Hampshire, a woodcut image of a ship from yesteryear, either going out to sea or run aground.

"Here you are!" they say, big New England smiles.

"Thank you, sir!" I am grateful. All is forgiven. I take our travel documents gently, as if they are scrolls which will crumble on contact.

Lizzy says nothing. Later, Lizzy will say, "Why do you thank them for what is yours by right?"

"Take the HOV lane," the patrolmen say, "it's on us."

But the last thing we're going to do is take the HOV lane.

"We sure will!" I say anyway.

And just like that Lizzy and I are across the New Hampshire border, the toy car getting smaller in the rearview mirror, my foot on the pedal, Lizzy continuing to mutter beside me in the passenger seat.

"Do you see?" she says. "*Now* do you see what this has come to?"

"We have our stamps, don't we?" I say.

"That's the point," she says.

"*What's* the point?" I say.

"It will be gone before you know it!" Her voice is rising, and to emphasize the importance of her words she bangs her fist four times on the center console trimmed in wood: *it. will. be. gone.* Here she might also be referring to *us*.

"What is that supposed to mean?" I say.

"It means that this is just the beginning!" she says.

I'm still not sure what this means.

"First states," she says, "then cities!"

Now she's screaming. Not at me, at society. Society in general. She's stuffing our stamped and precious paperwork back into the glove compartment.

"Be careful!" I say.

"Paperwork can't break!" she says.

She slams the glove compartment closed and it pops right back open. She slams it again.

"The glove compartment," I say, "*that* can break!"

"What do you care?" she says. "You don't own this car!"

"It's on my credit card," I say.

"No," she says, "it's on *our* credit card."

So this is going to be the first fight of the trip, and I have the inclination to go ahead and take the HOV lane after all, just to be spiteful. Instead, I split the difference and turn the leather steering wheel hard, swerving down the back road, going fifty in a twenty-five zone, dirt kicking up around the Escalade, speeding past some town named Ossipee, population four digits, which probably doesn't have an inn, and beyond which is the New Hampshire countryside, indistinguishable from the Maine countryside, bucolic and watercolored, breathtaking really, where a single peach stand comes into view, first distant, then immediate, a rare sign of life, two tables long, manned by a family of Ossipees and loaded with fruit the size of orange softballs.

"Look," we say, "peaches!"

Oh, but who would I be without Lizzy? Or more to the point, who would I *become* without her? I had never done yoga until we'd met. I had never drunk green tea. I had never contemplated society. "I've never eaten an avocado," I'd confided in her one afternoon, standing in front of an avocado display at the natural food store, six weeks into our relationship. She must have sensed my shame and embarrassment, thirty years old and so unworldly. "Don't blame yourself," she'd said, "blame your parents." I'd appreciated her compassion. I'd appreciated how she'd regarded this minor oversight about food as symptomatic of larger oversights in my childhood. I'd never considered my childhood.

She'd bought six avocados right there on the spot, good parent that she was, and later we sat cross-legged on her living room floor, amid the iconography of ancient goddesses as she sliced one open with a paring knife, slowly, sexually, cutting into the soft flesh just for me. I thought it would taste like an olive, given its giant pit, but it tasted like unsalted butter at room temperature. When we kissed, she told me, "I've never really been loved before." Indeed, she'd had the opposite of love, mostly in the form of an alcoholic college professor for a father who had once chased her around the living room with a frying pan while her enabling mother watched from the armchair, so blaming parents came easy for her. "Love can't exist under these conditions," she'd said. I wasn't sure if she was talking about her parents or society. We were three months into the relationship when I moved into her apartment with twenty cardboard boxes and a full-sized futon, almost big enough for two people. We commingled our finances, we applied for a joint credit card, we paid our bills from the joint credit card. We made dinner each night from scratch, kneading bread, simmering broth, crushing spices with mortar and pestle. "Slow cooking," she'd said. One evening I accidentally dropped a jar of molasses from the uppermost shelf in the kitchen. It fell and shattered, oozing like lava across the floor. We watched and laughed, marveling at its incremental, almost imperceptible progress, and it was only afterward that I thought how we should have seen this, not as comedy, but as the first sign of ailment sent from the ancient goddesses, if you believed in that sort of thing. "I love you," I told her, standing in the kitchen, the molasses twelve inches from our feet, but hours away. "Do you mean it?" she said. She got serious. "Do you really mean it?" "Yes, I mean it," I said. And I did mean it. And I still do.

But four states later we haven't had sex. Not in the Motel 6. Not in the Best Western. Not in the Hilton Garden Inn, which is not an inn or a garden, and which, halfway through Pennsylvania, we decide to splurge on spur-of-the-moment, designed as it is for an even higher-end traveling executive in mind, because let's live a little. Lizzy and I drink the complimentary bottled water and wrap ourselves in the bathrobes, and we lie together on the king-sized bed, as we do every night, our fingers intertwined, considering the popcorn ceiling, having been subdued and sedated by the Cadillac Escalade. In the morning we wake at dawn and pack up the free hotel toiletries and drive onward below the speed limit, taking the long way through society, wary of what might have changed for the worse, but noticing nothing, unless nothing *is* something. When we do see other cars, the license plates are always of the state we are in. Pennsylvania, Pennsylvania, Pennsylvania. Ohio, Ohio, Ohio. Still, we go deeper. Five, six, seven states. We eschew the landmarks for the lesser known: the streams, the bluffs, the mom-and-pops, the farm-to-tables, the things that will be gone, according to Lizzy, before we know it. Speaking of the mom-and-pops, they are the ones who have become wary, as have the farm-to-tables, as have the peach stands. They are concerned. They are skeptical. They are fascinated. "Where are you from?" they want to know. "Where are you headed?" We tip big to show we're just regular people on vacation. Later, Lizzy tells me, "This is how society is changing." She gets melancholy about this. When we fill up for gas, which is every day, the gas station attendants will ask, "Where are you from?" But generally the gas stations are self-serve.

By the time we get to Iowa we have lost track of what we've seen and where we've seen it, the landscape of the country transforms so gradually that it's only one hundred miles after the fact when we realize mountains have given way to cornfields have given way to plains. "Remember that river?" we say to each other. "Remember that lake?" Which state was that lake? Illinois? Rhode Island? New York? We can't recall. Lizzy says, "What difference does it make what state was that lake? States are random delineations anyway." There is truth to this, of course, but at each border we stop and show our travel documents, and at each border we are waved through by the patrolmen, no questions, no problems, New Hampshire apparently having been the exception to the rule.

"Have a good trip," the patrolmen say to us, barely glancing at our travel documents, now stamped with the seals of a dozen states, mostly images of frigates and agricultural implements.

"We hope you come back," they say. "You're welcome here anytime," they say.

"See?" I say to Lizzy.

"See what?" she says.

"See things are not so bad."

She says nothing. She places our precious travel documents in the glove compartment. She closes it with care.

"So why do you thank them," she asks, "for what is yours by right?"

In Kansas we decide to really splurge spur-of-the-moment and book a room at the Marriott, ten stories, ultramodern, sheathed in glass, room service, turndown service, also whirlpool on the ground floor. I withdraw my joint credit card with a flourish and the clerk swipes it once, twice, three times and tells me it's been *declined*.

"Must be a mistake," I say.

"Must be a mistake," Lizzy says.

"Must make a phone call," the clerk says.

"Yes," I say, "must make a phone call."

"Yes," the clerk says, "must be a mistake."

But I know it's no mistake. Lizzy knows it, too. So does the clerk. We have deferred too long. Now Lizzy and I try to save face and come up with cash to pay for the night, along with our checking account information to cover minibar incidentals, of which there will be none. I fill out even more forms than I did for our travel documents, signing and initialing everywhere. "I've never done this before," the clerk says, as if he's engaged in an interesting experiment that he'll be able to tell his buddies about. Twenty minutes later, Lizzy and I are anticlimactically granted the keycard that will get us into the room that we can't afford, Room 814, top floor and bittersweet, designed not so much for traveling executives than for traveling royalty, with shear drapes, wood floors, Neutrogena toiletries, no bad art, no popcorn ceiling. Tonight Lizzy and I do not lie on our backs unwinding silently on the king-sized bed, instead we get ready to go straight to sleep, ignoring the bathrobes and the imperial opulence, ignoring each other, mustering our energy for "the talk" that we both know we are going to have tomorrow, the talk about the joint credit card, which I am sure, even as I step naked into the shower with the frosted glass and the marble walls, won't be a talk but a *fight*, and it won't be about the credit card but about us, and what ails us, what has always ailed us, which we've only ever deferred.

We can go slow no longer. In the morning we take the turnpike, paying the toll with loose change, which clinks with the ring of indigence. "They should be paying *us*," Lizzy says. How she has come to this conclusion, I do not know. Immediately the unrelenting sameness of the country sets in, the crushing loss of distinction, the absolute homogeneity, the straight line of asphalt. No bluffs, no shoppes, no mom-and-pops. No watercolors from days of yore. Lizzy is right, they will be gone before we know it. I'm doing sixty-five in a sixty-five zone, fast is the new slow, the Cadillac Escalade hurtling earthward like a projectile. Kansas, Kansas, Kansas, say the license plates. Lizzy is arguing out loud beside me, saying something about turnpikes and big boxes and hollow calories. Somehow they're all connected. "Whatever happened to family-owned?" she says. "Whatever happened to DIY? Whatever happened to washing your clothes in the river?" I can tell she's just getting started and that she'll keep listing things all the way to the Nebraska border, where she will finally conclude with, Whatever happened to beating our rugs with a broom?

"Do you know who's to blame?" she asks me.

No, I do not know who is to blame. I am tired and confused. Mainly I am angry, mostly at her for having convinced me to break the bank with this Cadillac Escalade which we both knew full well we could not afford and which will now pursue us at top speed for years to come by way of a maxed-out monthly credit card statement, of which we will only ever be able to pay the minimum.

"Yes, I do know who's to blame," I say. "*You're* to blame!" But I don't say it, I shout it, at the top of my lungs, while banging on the center console with my fist to emphasize my words: *you're. to. blame.* And she's yelling and banging, too, and we're going through every fight we've ever had, like the time she left the empty jar of tomato sauce in the refrigerator, and the time I broke the bathroom light bulb after she'd just replaced it, every fight that will lead straight to this fight in the pristine confines of the Escalade. "Ten years for what?" Lizzy is asking me. But she's not asking, she's *stating.* She's cataloging every one of her grievances, each one still fresh in her mind, recalling them in vivid detail as if they'd just happened, especially the missed opportunities. She's yelling and then she's sobbing. Yelling *while* she's sobbing, trying to get the words out, but they're garbled, but I can understand her anyway, we don't need language anymore. And soon she's stopped doing an inventory of her slights, and begun doing one of her *life*, big picture, where it's been, where it's going, which is nowhere, really. "It's too late for me at forty," she keeps saying. Even in the midst of the chaos and rage, I want to assure her that this isn't true, that slow living has been good to her, slow living, slow cooking, and that yoga has been good to her, too, Saraswati, that it's been a balm, that it's kept her young, that she still has a bright future ahead even in middle age. Who would she be without me, I had wondered. Why, she would be someone wonderful. I'm the one who should be concerned, balding, can barely touch my toes, diminishing chi. She's the one with hair that's brown and lush, scented with motel shampoo, and even though she has the onset of crow's-feet, they're only noticeable when you stare at the side of her face from two feet away, like I've been doing for however many miles.

And it is right then that I become aware that I'm being followed by the border patrol in an unmarked, unremarkable sedan, four-door and white, the kind, in hindsight, we would have been better off renting from that eighteen-year-old summer employee at Hertz. It's been following us for the last fifty miles or so, constant in my rearview, strangely always about a half car's length away, closer than what you're taught in driver's ed, and whose presence has suddenly wound its way up into my consciousness as a thing about which I need to be aware.

"Who is that?" Lizzy asks. She has stopped shouting.

And as if in response, the border patrolmen put on their high beams, shooting straight through the hatchback of the Cadillac Escalade and over three rows of empty seats, lighting up the interior, sunshine notwithstanding, the universal sign for pull over, which I do, on the side of the turnpike, putting the car in park and popping the glove compartment open.

"*Now* do you see?" Lizzy says. She knows she's won.

Now we wait, our precious travel documents in hand, the white sedan idling behind us, one long stream of cars passing by at sixty-five miles an hour, everything a blur. Kansas, Kansas, Kansas. I should be focused on the border patrol, but I'm focused on the fight and the sadness, and the feeling that we are in a place in our relationship, Lizzy's and mine, from which there is no going back. And it also occurs to me, far too late of course, that we are not actually waiting at the border, nor anywhere near the border, but rather in the middle of the state, and that the white sedan is not the border patrol, but something of which I should have long been wary.

When the car door opens I am momentarily relieved to see that exiting the sedan are two old men, somewhere between avuncular and grandpa, dressed in loafers and khakis, ambling toward the Cadillac Escalade as if on their way to a picnic on the side of the turnpike.

I roll down the window. "Hello," I call, and this is where the avuncular ends and the menace begins.

"What are you doing here?" they want to know. There are no smiles. There is no Midwest goodness.

"No business," I say, upbeat and reassuring, "just personal."

"That's not what we asked you," they say.

"What gives you the right to ask us anything?" Lizzy says. Which is the wrong thing to ask, because they pull me shirt-first from the car, nearly dragging me along the pavement, some combination of pushing and pulling. They are surprisingly strong for being so old, and even in the midst of my distress, I wonder if I will be as strong as they are when I am their age, if ever I am.

"I have travel documents, sir!" I say, my voice at a high pitch. Lizzy's directive to always maintain dignity now a distant theory.

They don't care about the travel documents. They don't care about the border patrol. They don't care about the green tea in the cooler.

"Do we look like the border patrol?" they ask me. They sound insulted.

No, they look like they could be the regional managers for the Motel 6, and somehow I know that this makes things much worse.

I can hear Lizzy shouting from the front seat, Stop, stop, stop, and the cars whooshing past, the passengers staring out and wondering, briefly, what that man must have done so wrong, and I have a vision of running through the underbrush of Kansas, poor wayward fool, being chased by old men in loafers.

"Concerned citizens of Kansas," they tell me. I can't tell if this is an organization or a figure of speech.

"I'm not a drinker, sir," I say, because perhaps they're concerned that I've been driving through their state under the influence.

But they don't care about drinking and driving.

"What's wrong with your own state?" they ask me.

"The zigzag route," is all I can think to say.

They have me up hard against the hood of the Cadillac Escalade, which is covered in the dust and dead insects of a thousand back roads. Still, the beautiful crimson shines through, cherry-red in the sunlight, painted so skillfully that there is no evidence of even a single brushstroke.

LAST MEAL AT WHOLE FOODS

'm having dinner at the Whole Foods on Center Boulevard with my mother, who is dying. My poor mother, whom I'm trying not to sob over, is sitting across from me in the booth, transfixed by her cardboard plate, eating, with a strange and elegant enthusiasm, broccoli cake and something or other, as if any of this mattered.

She's still a young woman, which is half the tragedy, and she had me too young, which is the other half of the tragedy, but she remains beautiful, even close to death, with her hair mostly blond and her face almost flawless. If a stranger were to walk past our table he might mistake us for an attractive couple on a date; her beauty is a vexing and unresolved public issue for me. Now I sit in fear that at any moment the plastic fork will snap off between her teeth.

How she has maintained an appetite I have no idea. She's always been a nibbler because her figure has always been paramount, long legs and a narrow waist—even during her years of celibacy—but in the wake of the dire and unexpected news her hunger has become voracious. Perhaps it was just lying in wait. Meanwhile, the brown rice and assorted greens on my cardboard plate have grown cold. No matter, I'll eat later at the all-night diner near my house which serves whatever the opposite of brown rice and assorted greens is. My own sustenance is the least of my concerns at present. Everything is the least of my concerns at present. Everything except the ticking of the clock that has begun its final countdown. In contrast to the short time that remains for my mother stands the long time that remains for me. This long time includes everything that I must do during and after her short time. Dying is arduous and taxing. Only the dead rest in peace.

I'd taken the afternoon off from work so that I could accompany my mother to her doctor's appointment, which, given all available evidence, was supposed to be a mere formality. We had even laughed about it. "Test results, ha-ha." Now all bets were off. "The next few months are going to be the most challenging," the doctor had told us. He made it sound as if he were delivering moderately good news, as if there were less challenging months to come, and if we could only get through these "next few months" it would be smooth sailing after that. What he really meant was that at some point soon my mother would be dead and the challenge would be over. That was the silver lining. That was what my mother and I had to look forward to.

Twenty years ago, we wouldn't have been eating at a Whole Foods on Center Boulevard. Twenty years ago, commuters driving in from the suburbs gave the street a wide berth on their way downtown, even if it added fifteen, twenty, thirty minutes to their trip. They referred to this as "doing the loop," and it turned into a joke, and then it turned into a song by a local rock band that became popular on the radio station. The only reason to come to Center Boulevard back then was if you were the type of person who needed to shop at Goodwill. My mother and I each happened to be that type of person.

Six days in the city and we had no dishes. So we set out one morning, naïve and holding hands, and when we finally came around the corner, forty-five minutes later, we were greeted by a long and unlucky road, running all the way to the horizon, bounded on both sides by burned-out buildings and exhibiting no signs of life. There wasn't even a parked car. The emptiness was overwhelming, and so was the silence—we could hear our own footsteps on the pavement. If my mother was nervous she didn't show it; even her hand in mine remained perspiration-free. Way off in the distance was the big blue Goodwill sign beckoning us with its half a smiling face. "Ooh, there it is!" my mother said, as if we were in the culminating stages of a treasure hunt. Midway to our destination a man came darting out from between two buildings. He was shirtless, even though it was late fall, and he stood in our path staring at us, saying nothing, breathing hard. After a few moments of panting, he gave my mother a wink, a gesture I didn't completely understand, and then he disappeared back where he'd come from. It happened so quickly that it was hard to know if it had happened at all. My mother said sympathetically, "Looks like that man could use a shirt from Goodwill," but it felt as if she were talking about something we'd seen in a movie a long time ago.

We ended up spending the entire afternoon browsing the dregs, before purchasing two pots and a chipped dining set for three that smelled of mothballs. There was no three, of course, but it was smart to be prepared for all eventualities. And since I'd been "such a good boy today," my mother bought me, as a token of her appreciation, a football jersey of the local team. It had yellow stripes and blue stars and a stain on the sleeve. I was eight years old and didn't know anything about football. "It fits you perfectly," she said, and it did. On the back was a strange, unpronounceable name in large white letters. I had become someone named

Kruszewski. I felt like a clown. "You'll learn all about it soon enough," she said. She was trying to be upbeat, and I didn't want to disappoint her. She wanted to spin this move to a new city as just one in a series of adventures, when in fact it was a last-gasp attempt at finding our own goodwill.

But she was right: the football jersey somehow made me an instant star among my classmates. Kruszewski happened to be the best player on the league's worst team, and, merely by wearing the shirt, I was closely associated with him. I even managed to affect a tone of authority when discussing the previous week's game, which I hadn't seen and wouldn't have understood if I had. All I had to do was let others narrate while I reenacted the highlights by falling on the floor and rolling around with general fervor.

Eventually I learned the rules and became a fan, and for a while a rumor went around class, precipitated mostly by my mysterious arrival in the middle of the school year, that I might actually be Kruszewski's son. I did nothing either to encourage or to dispel this rumor. It was tantalizing for everyone, including me, to think that I might actually be the child of a star. "I'm not saying yes," I would say with world-weariness, "and I'm not saying no." No, I was the son of an engineering professor who was bald and smoked a pipe, whose only foray into physical exertion was the summer of his sophomore year of college, when he washed dishes in the campus cafeteria. He confided in me once, wistfully, while extolling the virtues of manual labor, that

he "had even begun to develop some muscles that summer." I understood this to be mainly a cautionary tale, no
doubt because those muscles had subsequently been lost,
never to be rediscovered, and because, perhaps as compen-
sation, he spent the greater part of my childhood holed up
in his bachelor pad making love to a succession of engineering students, plying them with sweet nothings about their
scientific genius. That was what he had plied my mother
with until he got her pregnant. The party was over for him
after that, or at least it was on hiatus for the next five years,
until he could figure out a way to extricate himself from
her. Her meaning my mother. After the cleaving, he made
sure to send money. The money was in lieu of visiting me.
"I'm sure you can appreciate how overwhelmed I am with
committee work," he scribbled on official letterhead, which
my mother saved in a shoebox. The checks came frequently
at first, then haphazardly, then hardly at all. "I'm sure you
can appreciate the limitations of a professor's salary." My
mother found a job at the neighborhood library, "a way
station," she called it, all the while dreaming of one day
becoming an engineer and designing roller coasters. On the
weekends, she'd clear off the kitchen table and unfurl dusty
blueprints from her college days. They were all numbers
and arrows, and I couldn't see any suggestion of an actual
roller coaster.

"Where's the fun?" I asked.

"The fun is coming," she said.

———

Now Kruszewski is long retired and there's a Whole Foods on Center Boulevard and my mother is dying. Across from the Whole Foods is Starbucks. Next to Starbucks is Penelope's Boutique. Next to the boutique is another boutique, and so on, for the length of the boulevard, the sequence interrupted only by the Goodwill, the sole remaining evidence of the age when this boulevard was a wasteland inhabited by shirtless phantasms. The blue sign still beckons with its smiling half face that looks as if it had been drawn by a child with a crayon, but now it beckons the hip, who go there to discover cheap vintage clothes that a poor person would never dare wear. The Goodwill will outlast Whole Foods; I'm sure of it. It'll outlast Starbucks, too. When the boulevard crumbles and reverts to its genuine self, Goodwill will be the last man standing. That's the cycle.

My mother pauses long enough in eating her broccoli cake to take an extended drink of water from a plastic cup. Her head goes back and her throat contracts gracefully. "Mmm," she says with appreciation, as if she'd just come in from a hot day in the fields. Perhaps when your days are numbered your senses become heightened and you begin to experience everything with newfound intensity. After all, how many more drinks of water are left for her? How many more meals at Whole Foods? The march toward finiteness has begun. She wipes her mouth with her napkin, leaving one lone crumb on her chin, and I want to say, politely,

Mom, maybe you should, you know, wipe your face again, because she has always been mortified by even one piece of lint on her dress. When I was a child, she would screech and recoil anytime my finger approached the vicinity of my nose. But more pressing issues have usurped the lifelong primacy of good manners. Good manners, good graces, good looks have become things of the past. We've arrived at that realm where the physical body has decreed an entirely new set of rules of acceptability.

"Do you want something else?" I ask. There's a plaintive tone to my voice.

She looks at me and smiles. She licks her red lips. I wonder if her lips are drying out, and if this is an indication of the disease working its way toward the surface. Her demeanor betrays nothing of the verdict we're contending with. I feel traumatized, as if I'd just walked away from a plane crash, but her legs are crossed and her posture's perfect. Her earrings catch the fluorescent light.

"Yes," she says, "there is something else I want." Emphasis on "else," emphasis on "want." She leans toward me. She smells faintly of perfume. I can tell she's thinking not in the narrow sense of wanting something else *tonight*, like broccoli cake, but in the terrifying existential sense of wanting something else from *life*. For most of my childhood there was always something more we wanted, something more we were just about to get, something that was going to turn our situation around once and for all. It was vague and indefinable, this thing, hovering nearby in the air. I had relied on my mother to get us that thing, but there was only so much she could do, and now we have only three months left to do it.

But no, I'm wrong, she just wants more broccoli cake.

That night, in order to pass some of our precious time, we play a game of Scrabble, sitting by the wood-burning fireplace that my mother restored at great expense after I finished college and moved out. It's August and it's hot and there's no reason to start a fire, but it seems fitting somehow that we spend our last days together enjoying the warmth of a fireplace that sat vacant and defunct throughout my childhood. This portal into the world was the stuff of troubling dreams for me. How could we be so certain that someone or something wouldn't descend into our home in the middle of the night?

"Don't be ridiculous," my mother had told me, misunderstanding my concern. "Santa Claus is a myth."

I can see myself looking back at this game of Scrabble years from now, looking back at myself looking back, Mom and me, sitting on the rug as the flames licked, the wood cracked, the heat emanated. It's the type of memory one should make an effort to create if one has the opportunity. In a few short months I will be selling this house, including the fireplace, which, I suppose, has added some value to what is, at best, a modest two-bedroom, two-story home with some original fixtures in a mildly decent neighbor-hood. But now is not the time to think of things like real estate. Now is the time to think of *moments*. Our *moments* together in this house. The rug I sit on, the Samsung televi-sion I used to watch, the couch in the corner, all the famil-iar objects from the past—these I will sell on Craigslist.

"Maybe I should start a fire," I say, as if the thought had just flitted through my mind.

And to my surprise my mother agrees, perhaps discern-ing that we have entered the territory of the profound. "Okay," she says, "that sounds like a nice idea."

Nice idea, indeed. Except I can't quite remember how to get a fire going. I can't remember, because I never learned. I fumble with the logs and the lighter fluid and the bellows. The flame catches but does not hold. It dwindles to noth-ing. My mother has to come and help, and now the two of us are struggling side by side. "Like *this*," she tells me with frustration, because she is, if nothing else, an impa-tient person in the face of what she deems foolishness. She could never tolerate grammatical errors on my homework or in my speech. She could not tolerate laziness or idiocy in me or in others. "You won't believe what So-and-So did today!" she'd say, regaling me with stories of her incompe-tent coworkers. Maybe she sensed that her own incompe-tence was lurking somewhere beneath the surface.

Then suddenly, out of an unforgiving slab of wood, a

flame comes to life, soft and yellow, just barely hanging on. Even from this small flame I can feel a significant amount of heat radiating, and I have an inkling that this nice idea of mine is actually a ridiculous idea, and that in a few minutes the living room will be sweltering, suffocating its occupants.

"How lovely," my mother says.

The Scrabble game is the same one we used when I was a child. It's missing one of the *f*'s and the board is so worn that it has almost come apart. We'd played on rainy days. "Dog," "cat," that type of thing. She was always encouraging and pedagogic. "What a good *verb*," she would say. She would assist me at the end of the game, that desperate, grueling time when one has only a few letters remaining, the majority of them vowels, and the board is already so crowded that there is no place to spell even the word "it." There was a humiliating quality to that endgame, having to have her come lean over and help, her breath on my neck. "Show Mommy your letters." I was a little boy being instructed in the immutable fact of my own helplessness. Here, then, was my first lesson. "Look!" she would say. " 'Rat' —'rate'!" It was a form of alchemy, this ability to dislodge hidden words. "Look: 'at'—'eat'!" She was too eager in her discoveries. Her eagerness compounded my powerlessness. When I looked down at the board to try to fend for myself, I could find nothing, anywhere. My mother's delight in wordplay infuriated me, and on one occasion I slammed my fist into the middle of the board, upsetting two hours' worth of spelling.

Now it is my mother who, on her first three turns, is spelling things like "at" and "or," saying *tsk-tsk* to herself, garnering three points per turn, shrugging as if it were all just the luck of the draw, as if the game only ever came down to whatever random letters you happened to choose. The letters are the letters, her *tsk-tsk* implies, and there is nothing more you or anyone else could have done differently. Her inability to spell is troubling, and I worry that it is in fact a result of the illness worming its way into her brain, overtaking the part of the mind that processes vocabulary. I have a desire to rush to her side and show her what she could have spelled for fourteen points. "Look, Mom, here: 'mouse'!" This would be something I would look back on and see as our lives having come full circle. Or perhaps my mother just doesn't care about spelling anymore. Why struggle, she has decided, why labor, why churn when there are only a few weeks to go? This competitiveness has always been so silly. Let's just spell "be" and move on with it so we can sit here enjoying each other's company in front of the fireplace.

But I can't move on. I have resolved to produce something brilliant with what I've been given: aamasjp. I will not be dissuaded from this cause. My unconscious, ever more astute than my conscious, is sending a faint signal not

to give up, that a seven-letter word does indeed exist somewhere within the jumble. I am determined to uncover it. I
am determined to impress my mother. She will be able to
witness the fruits of her labor. She will kiss me on the face.
She will gush with praise for her little boy now all grown up
and a successful speller.

Time passes. I am aware of the time passing. I am aware
that the temperature in the living room is growing close
to unbearable. I've rolled up my sleeves. I've taken off my
socks. Droplets of sweat have broken out on my forehead
and neck. How long does it take a log to fully burn? To
put the fire out now, midway, would be to accept defeat, to
invite bad luck. When I glance at my mother she appears,
thankfully, to be indifferent both to the heat and to how
long I'm taking. She peers at her letters with curiosity. Even
in the heat she's composed, her cheeks just slightly flushed.

"Whose turn is it?" she wants to know. Her voice star-
tles me. It's been quiet for too long. Only the fire has been
making noise. I'm worried that her question is rhetorical
and that she is gently prodding me to spell my word, whatever it is—"map," "amp," "maps"—so that we can end this
childish game.

"It's my turn," I say. My voice is even more startling than
my mother's. I need water. I need air. But I can't stop now.
I'm close, I can feel that I'm close—my unconscious is telling me that the moment of truth is drawing near, and that
to stand up and open a window would be to jeopardize the

balance of forces in the room, and that to compromise with "map" would be to squander a final chance at everlasting glory, and, yes, suddenly there it is, yes, in a flash, staring up at me. My mind has unlocked the mystery, it has given rhythmic order to that paralyzing randomness that has been confronting me all evening: "pajamas."

"Here you go, Mom," I say, as modestly as I can, as if this were a favor done for her sake, my hands shaking as I lay down the seven wonderful letters that will reap me no less than eighty points. But Mom has fallen asleep, her head bent, her blond hair falling down around her face.

The next day I take a trip to Ellsworth Daybreak Vista, in the valley by the old skating rink, to inquire about reserving a room for my mother. Ellsworth Daybreak Vista could be your average, worn-out apartment building if it weren't for the two ambulances parked outside with their lights flashing. It's impossible to tell if they're coming or going, these ambulances, or are simply stationed there to wait for the inevitable. This is why I've chosen to come here without my mother—there's no reason to subject her to the grisly details of what lies in the future. Soon she will need everything: medicine at all hours, meals in bed, bathing, wiping, toenail-clipping. Any day now the minor things are going to become major things, and when everything falls apart it's going to fall apart fast.

The admissions coordinator greets me at the entrance. His name is Mickey Poindexter, and he's got a gut and a name tag and he smells like cigarettes. I think that I know him from somewhere, that we may have gone to the same high school, where he may have been one of those upper-classmen lunchtime assholes. But of this I can't be sure.

In any case, he's not an asshole anymore. "Welcome," he says. He grasps my hand warmly. "Right this way." He's concerned without being maudlin; he's comforting without being Pollyanna-ish. We all know why you're here, buddy, is the subtext. Let's do what we can to maintain our dignity.

We ride the elevator in respectful silence to the second floor, which can be accessed only by the turn of a key on Mickey's key chain. Entry and exit are obviously not at the discretion of the tenants. In other words, the tenants are not really tenants and this is not an apartment building. The elevator doors open onto six elderly people in wheelchairs watching a game show with their chins on their chests. An attendant sits nearby, her eyes glued to the screen, waiting for something exciting to happen. This is not the way to make a good first impression. There's a sign on the wall listing the weekly activities: chair exercises on Monday, etc. The carpeting, as anticipated, is worn and of a purple-green pattern that belongs to a different era, as does the wood paneling. Someone, I think, has soiled himself or herself recently, because the air is heavy with Febreze.

Mickey's office needs Febreze, too: it reeks of cigarette smoke. This makes me wonder if he sits in here chain-smoking all day, and, if so, what other rules does he flout? Football paraphernalia covers the walls, floor-to-ceiling, the yellow stripes and blue stars of past teams, going so far back in time that there's even a framed pair of socks from when the team was blue stripes and yellow stars. We break the ice by talking about the upcoming season, which happens to begin tonight, with the first, meaningless preseason game. Mickey is full of facts and figures. I don't know what he's talking about. I gave up on the team years ago, because one can endure only so much defeat before it begins to feel like a manifestation of one's own character. The last time I went to a game I was sixteen, standing outside the stadium for hours with three of my friends, hoping to get autographs. The team had lost again, and the players, when they finally emerged from the tunnel, were gloomy. Still, they signed. Thirty years, and there hadn't been a championship. Thirty years, and they hadn't even come close. But each year was a new beginning, each year was the year it was finally going to happen. "Why not us?" was the slogan one season, plastered on billboards and the sides of buses. It was a good question with no good answer.

But according to Mickey things are now lining up perfectly. Apparently we've made the right trades, and we've signed the right free agents, we've cut the right washed-up players. This is our year, he says. This is *supposed* to be our year. He's adamant. He's passionate. He's in love. I want to remind him that every year is supposed to be our year, and every year ends up being someone else's year, but he speaks with such optimism and insight that his conviction is infectious. He may make a believer of me again, which isn't hard, since deep down we all want to be believers. "Start watching them tonight," he says with confidence. Meanwhile, I ooh and aah over the memorabilia he's accumulated throughout the years. No memorabilia too obscure. Case in point: he has a single silver cleat, the size of a tooth, that broke off from one of the players' shoes during a game.

"I bought it for three hundred and fifty dollars," Mickey tells me proudly. It seems a fair price.

Speaking of fair price, the room for my mother will cost four thousand a month, not including laundry service. I'm wondering if our rapport over football will earn me some kind of break.

"Will she need her clothes laundered?" Mickey wants to know. His voice is concerned and comforting.

"Yes," I say. "Yes, she will."

That's an additional forty-five dollars.

We take the elevator to the third floor by way of Mickey's key chain. Above the third floor is the fourth floor. Above the fourth floor is the fifth floor. The fifth floor is where tenants go when they lose their minds. There is no sixth floor.

"This is our nicest floor," Mickey assures me, referring to the floor we are walking on.

I don't know what makes this the nicest floor, but I'm beginning to suspect that Mickey might be the best salesman I've ever met. The thought makes me suspicious. It also makes me susceptible. The hallway is long and has the same purple-green carpeting as the second floor, but here it seems more vibrant—stylish, even. We turn and turn again. We pass a nurses' station, where two nurses are standing hip to hip, as if on an assembly line, divvying up the day's doses. Apart from the four of us, there is no indication that there are any actual living people on this floor. Hanging on the doors are signs that say things like WE LOVE YOU, GRANDPA, but these feel as if they were messages written long ago. I wonder if I will make a sign for my mother's door. I wonder if I will come and play Scrabble with her. I wonder how long her stay here will be, and I do some quick math in my head in multiples of four thousand.

Room 303, our final destination, is not accessed by way of a key. The door is open and the Febreze is evident. How long has this room been vacant, and what is the Febreze intended to disguise? Three-oh-three seems like a number that has, or should have, some symbolic significance in my mother's life, but I can draw no connection.

Mickey stands to the side, as any good Realtor knows to do, allowing me to take in the surroundings as if I had walked in on my own. It's a small, quiet, square room with a kitchenette and a window that faces the courtyard, where a tree is in full bloom. I make a big deal about the tree, the leaves, the branches, and this pleases Mickey, as if he had planted it himself. I hope that my mother, the librarian, will be satisfied with the tranquility. I hope she will say that I did a good job of finding this, her final home. I hope that she will not resent me.

"Here's the walk-in closet," Mickey says proudly.

There's no need whatsoever for a walk-in closet. My mother will come with barely enough to fill a dresser. I want to tell Mickey to seal up the walk-in closet and knock five hundred dollars off the rent. Close off the kitchenette, too. Just keep the two nurses in the nurses' station—everything else is superfluous and ostentatious. Even the window that faces the courtyard can go. Even the tree.

That evening I make a serious error in judgment and take my mother to see *Life of Pi*. In 3-D, no less. It's playing at the Royal Cineplex at the absurd price of three dollars and fifty cents, which makes me feel as if my decision were that much more sound.

"Why so cheap?" I ask the ticket-taker.

"We aim to please," he says. He's about nineteen, and he's showing off for my mother. When she walks past, he looks at her butt.

The ticket price harks back to an earlier era, an era that

predates me, an era in which my mother and father would have flourished, all uncomplicated technology, clear rules, understandable roles. I thought *Life of Pi* would reflect that era as well, simpleminded storytelling with a happy ending, but within thirty minutes there's a young man floating alone on a boat in the ocean with wild animals trying to kill him. The metaphor is robust and immediate. We've got two hours to go, my mother and I, with plastic glasses stuck to our faces. Violence, desperation, desolation fill the screen. Violence is one thing, but desolation is another. And desolation in 3-D is another still. The sea, where our hero must somehow make peace with the animals, floats off the screen toward me. I feel as if I'm about to drown beneath this false water.

Yet my mother appears captivated by what's unfolding. She leans forward in her seat, elbows on her knees, lights flashing off her glasses.

"Isn't this so boring?" I ask, as if it couldn't be anything but.

My mother shrugs. She's amenable to anything. Perhaps when you don't have much time left equanimity sets in and you spell "or" and you leave in the middle of movies, no questions asked. We exit the way we came, tossing our half-used glasses in the cardboard box. The ticket-taker gets one last chance to check out my mother.

On the way home we stop at the all-night diner by my

house for a cup of coffee and "maybe a bite to eat." There are six televisions above the counter, all tuned to the same channel: the preseason football game. The sound is off, but the mood in the diner is pure excitement. Two dozen fools sit jabbering, staring upward, watching the silent commentators analyze and extrapolate.

My mother wants broccoli cake, or some approximation of it, but the diner doesn't sell that, of course.

"We don't got any of that, hon," the waitress says. My mother flinches at the grammar.

In lieu of broccoli cake I order her a side of steamed broccoli, a slice of red-velvet cake, and some ice cream, because why not? The lights in the diner are bright, unflatteringly so, but still my mother looks young and beautiful. She'll always look young and beautiful. Even on her final day at Ellsworth Daybreak Vista her eyes will be blue and striking, her hair will be lush. She won't fall apart. She'll make sure of it.

I can see the televisions from where we're sitting, and on the first play of the game the wayward rookie, the one that everybody had been dubious about, takes the ball and races eighty yards into the end zone. "Look at that, Mom!" I say. The diner goes crazy, and my mother turns around to see what the fuss is about. And then, just a few plays later, our team scores again, and the patrons are screaming even louder, and now my mother is smiling and clapping, and so am I. And before that first quarter is over we've scored four more times. Everyone is standing and shouting, everyone including the waitress, including my mother, the diner full of fire and zeal, as if this lone preseason game had any bearing on what's to come.

A, S, D, F

By the time six o'clock is about to roll around, I'm beginning to wonder if working in an art gallery is taking some sort of a toll on my psyche. Part of the problem is that I haven't done anything all day since there hasn't been anything to do, and the other part of the problem is something I can't quite name yet. This is the moment when the owner emerges from his back office—three minutes before six—holding two pages of a handwritten letter that he needs me to type right now, because there's a collector on the West Coast who might be interested in *Untitled X*.

"One more thing before you go," he says, as if the list of today's tasks has been long.

"Sure thing," I tell him. I'm full of good cheer and work ethic. I was hired a month ago and I want the owner to think of me as a team player—but the truth is I don't get paid for overtime.

The truth is I've spent today the way I've spent most days, sitting behind the front desk for nine hours, less one hour for lunch, engulfed in a sea of silence and serenity, waiting for something to happen, while I gaze into the middle distance of white walls hung with abstract expressionism. This is the art of seventy years ago, the art of art, the art of ideas, the art of Rorschach, lines, shapes, splashes, repudiating verisimilitude and easy answers, 60 x 60, and selling for five figures if the owner's lucky. No, we don't have Pollocks or de Koonings, we have the ones no one's heard of, the ones that don't go for seven figures, and that don't hang in the Denver Art Museum where I worked in the café, before getting my act together to send out art-related résumés across the state of Colorado. "Executed optimal operations during peak hours," I wrote in my cover letter, poached business-speak off the Internet, but accurate nonetheless.

Today, the only visitor has been the mailman at noon, who put his big blue bag on my Formica front desk and spent a few minutes making small talk about sports and the weather, which was cloudless and cool, because in Aspen it's always cloudless and cool. A month ago I was

living in Denver where it was also cloudless and cool. The
mailman spoke too loudly for what's generally acceptable
in an upscale art gallery with a librarylike atmosphere—
"CLOUDLESS AND COOL"—but no one was here to
hear him. Before he left, I tried to get him to stay, saying
plaintively, "I can give you a personal tour if you like." I was
talking about the abstract expressionism on the walls, but
he thought I was talking about Aspen. "I've lived here my
whole life," he said.

Now it's six hours later, twelve past six to be exact, and
I'm doing my best, while suffering from workplace lassi-
tude, to type out two pages of a handwritten letter. What
I'm actually engaged in is a white-collar high-wire act without a safety net where each typo means I have to start over
with fresh stationery. If I was allowed to use the state-of-
the-art computer that's been staring at me all day in sleep
mode, I'd have finished ten minutes ago. Instead, I'm ham-
mering away on the manual typewriter, olive-green and
Smith Corona, circa the 1950s, which also happens to be
when the artwork on the walls is from. In other words, the
obsolete past.

"Dear _____:" the letter begins. "I believe I have
something in which you might be interested . . ."

The owner prefers a colon in the salutation, he prefers the
day of the month spelled out, "twenty-eighth," he prefers a
carbon copy filed alphabetically in the bottom drawer, the
original "cc" in red wax. He describes the painting's prov-

enance, its importance to modern art, its five-figure price,
which he wants spelled out. He's hovering by my desk as
I type, dressed in his three-piece suit and denim smock,
the embodiment of where art meets commerce, although
as far as I can tell it's been more art than commerce of
late. His presence is causing me consternation, but if he's
noticed that I'm on my third piece of letterhead, he seems
not to care. He's a good guy; he hired me, after all. "I like
your background," he'd told me during my job interview.
He was referring to two years in the Denver Art Museum,
never mind that it was food service. What he really liked
was that I came recommended by the father of a friend
of a friend, speaking of nepotism. I'm four removed from
power, meaning that I've been given an entry-level position
as a front-desk receptionist without having done much to
earn it. As for the owner, he's been in this business thirty
years, starting from nothing except an innate ability to "see
art," and he's worked his way up to where he is today.

"'Seeing' is not the same as 'looking,'" he'd said. I pretended I understood the distinction.

When I'm done typing the letter it's six-thirty, but time
doesn't matter to the owner. He reads the final copy twice,
handling the paper carefully, admiring his turns of phrase,
and then he does what he always does, measures the top
and bottom margins with the ruler he carries in his denim

smock. He's used to dealing in tenths of centimeters and percentages of UV. Sometimes my margins are askew, but today they're flawless, and this makes him pleased, and this seems to be a good time to recommend, gently, that if I was able to type his correspondence with the two-thousand-dollar computer sitting on the front desk in sleep mode we wouldn't ever have to worry about things like imperfect margins again.

"It's done automatically," I tell him, like, *Isn't that neat.*

He shakes his head. "I don't want automatic," he says. Of course, he doesn't. He wants debossed type. He wants pigment on the page. He wants art from the past.

Then he signs his name in big looping script, full of hope, sealing it up for the mailman tomorrow at noon.

"Thank you," the owner says to me, and he retreats to his back office, and I file the carbon copy in the bottom drawer next to the petty cash, where I take out fifteen dollars for myself, because I don't get paid for overtime.

It's six forty-five and it's cloudless and cool. Whatever you've heard about the beauty of Aspen is all true: snowcapped mountains with golden light, etc. The streets are mostly empty but every person I pass shares the same healthy sheen that comes from having twenty-four-hour access to fresh air, pure water, unlimited optimism. No one knows me, but they smile anyway. In Denver, the streets were more crowded and the people smiled less. "You're going to love it in Aspen," one of the museum guards told me on my last day at the café. He was dressed in his wash-and-wear suit. He was fifty removed from power. He'd never been out of Denver, so what he said was theory. "I know I will," I said, but I'd never been out of Denver, either.

Now I'm strolling through town trying to love it, trying to shake off the last nine-plus hours inside the art gallery, less one hour for lunch. I've been staring at abstract expressionism for so long that when I close my eyes, I don't see an afterimage of the snowcapped mountains with golden light, I see how the artists would have depicted those snowcapped mountains: white, yellow, angle, triangle, yellow, white. Then they'd title it *Mountain*, hang it on the wall, and let the viewer ponder. Not mountain, but un-mountain. Not mountain, but *essence* of mountain. Suddenly I'm seeing everything through the prism of the abstract expressionist's paintbrush, the stores, the streets, the signs, each object disassembled to its component parts of color and form, even the smiling faces of the strangers who pass by me, white, white, white, and underneath it all is the soundtrack of the continuous clacking of the typewriter keys. This is what I mean when I say that I'm beginning to wonder if working in an art gallery is taking some sort of toll on my psyche.

On the corner of such-and-such street, between a locally owned bakery and a family-owned florist, is an independently owned bookstore, big bay window filled with books, sandwich-board sign on the sidewalk that eschews the tongue-in-cheek message for the no-nonsense, OPEN, but which I read as *o, p, e, n.* I've passed this bookstore before and I've always thought of going in. There's a young woman about my age exiting the store, she's wearing a skirt and heels, presumably for her office job, and carrying under her arm half a bagful of books, cash flow concerns not a problem. In the entranceway we have one of those socially awkward interchanges where we're both trying to sidestep each other, left, right, left, right. Her face is sunburned from days of cloudless skies. Or maybe she's just embarrassed. She stops and stares at me with her dark eyes, a brooding, penetrating stare, and for some reason the gallery owner's maxim comes back to me full force, "Seeing is not the same as looking."

No one is inside the store except the cashier, standing behind the counter, subsumed by silence, setting sunlight streaming through the big bay window. He's probably been gazing into the middle distance of book spines since nine o'clock this morning. "Hello," he says to me. *H, e, l, l, o.* I have the fleeting thought that I should do for him what the mailman did for me, make small talk, after which the cashier will offer a personal tour of his store.

But the store is tiny, it's musty, it's the opposite of Barnes & Noble. No tour needed here. Here are the history books, the political books, the tell-alls. Here is Stephen King, six shelves for him, six hundred volumes, *The Long Walk*,

The Dead Zone, to name two. The titles tell you everything you need to know about what you're going to find
inside—somebody in jeopardy—and so do the covers with
their giant font, bold colors, silhouetted figures. Stephen
King isn't writing with metaphor and misdirection, he's not
interested in posing questions about the nature of life or art
or society. The only questions the reader will be pondering
are who's going to die. Yes, this is the antidote I need to
help undo the last nine hours, a good book, a fun book, a
page-turner, something with straightforward prose, crystal-
clear storytelling, something that goes down easy. But
which of these six hundred volumes should I choose? The
covers might be similar, but the subjects are wide-ranging:
cats, dogs, clowns, authors, the list goes on. There's one
about little boys who are paralyzed and attacked by were-
wolves, and another about little boys who are killed and
come back from the dead, and there's yet another, the most
famous of all, about little boys with special powers living in
abandoned hotels being pursued by deranged men wielding mallets.

As I go from book to book, gauging and appraising, I'm
getting the sense that I'm being watched by the cashier, ten
feet away behind the counter, increasingly suspicious, displeased, small-town smile gone, patience gone, too, about
to call out to me, No more browsing! Let's make a selection!
But no one talks like this in Aspen, of course. In Aspen, you
can stay as long as you like, friend, browse as long as you

like. You can thumb through all six shelves until your mind
has become so saturated with themes of violence and horror and degradation that you're no longer even in the right
section, but have unwittingly drifted into self-help, which,
oddly, has been placed next to Stephen King. These covers
are different, naturally, with thinner type, lighter colors,
sometimes stock photos, and they have titles like *a practical guide* or *a workbook*. I am far away from art now, and
I'm even farther from metaphor and misdirection. But the
theme of Stephen King remains the same: Somebody in
jeopardy. Depression, drug addiction, domestic violence.
Who will cope? Who will recover? Who will be alive by
the end? Come to think of it, it makes sense to have placed
self-help next to Stephen King, two selections of horror side
by side, one lived, one imagined. Death, disease, demen-
tia. I'm not even sure what I'm looking for anymore. Still,
I gauge and appraise, plucking at random one more book
from the very top shelf with a title that I'm able to render
only by its component parts: *boys. abused. sexually.*

The big bay window is behind me, but I can tell that the
sun has set on the snowcapped mountains. I can hear that
the cashier is getting ready to go home, rustling and bus-
tling. The book in my hand resembles all the other books,
innocuous font on white cover, but the stock photo of a
figure alone in a room, casting an impossibly long shadow,
calls to mind Stephen King. The author is Dr. So-and-So,
Ph.D., and he hasn't written "a practical guide" or "a work-

book," but rather, according to the doctor, "an investigation into the long-lasting impact," his words. He writes, at least in the preface, with an authority that I find tactless. He presumes to know his reader. He has the credentials to prove it. "Twenty-five years of clinical research," he says. In summary, his assessment is unflinching: symptoms, everything; prognosis, grim. He claims he has the statistics to prove it. If there's optimism in this book, the people of Aspen will have to slog through three hundred pages to find it.

Basically, what the doctor is suggesting is that you shouldn't be wasting your time with make-believe stories about boys being pursued through abandoned hotels by men wielding mallets—speaking of metaphor. What you really need to be doing is "coming to terms," and you need to be doing it now. You have to start figuring out how the obsolete past is interfering with the inescapable present, ten, fifteen, twenty years later, particularly how it's interfering with your attempt at happiness. But the main impediment, as far as the doctor's concerned, is that you don't know how to figure any of this out, and the other impediment is that you don't know if you want to.

This is when the cashier calls out, "Closing time," in a voice so mellifluous, so apologetic, and for a moment I'm able to glimpse an abstract expressionist view of myself, where I've been reduced to my own component parts, standing bleary-eyed in a bookstore, a long way from home, sun having set, crumpled in my pocket fifteen dollars of ill-gotten gains. Beneath it all, I can hear the clacking of the typewriter as Stephen King pounds out yet one more bestseller on horror.

The next day is cloudless and cool and all the streets by the funicular have been closed because Shaun White is in town. He's just won some major snowboarding championship—I don't follow his career—and now he's come to Aspen with his flowing red hair to shoot a Pepsi commercial or a video game or "a show for Netflix," someone in the crowd is saying. Anyone's guess is as good as anyone's. There are trucks and cables and cones, and a production assistant is standing in the intersection, arms folded, telling us we have to wait to cross the street. He likes telling us this. But when the light turns green, we still can't go, and then it turns green again, and if it turns green one more time I'm going to be late getting back to the art gallery from lunch. Someone's asking the production assistant if Shaun White is on the funicular now, if he's coming down the mountain in one of the cable cars jiggling at three miles an hour, about to make an impromptu appearance. The production assistant has no idea. "I just do what they tell me," he says. He's one hundred degrees removed from Shaun White.

There's a little girl sitting on top of her mother's shoulders, pointing up at the mountain, a ninety-degree slope of green topped with white, saying, "I can see Shaun White,

Mommy!" No, she can't. She's craning her neck, shielding her eyes against the unchanging Aspen sky. She wants to get up the mountain. She wants to meet Shaun White. "Can I, Mommy?" she asks. She reminds me of my own unrestrained excitement when I was her age, specifically with a certain Denver skyscraper where my mother worked as a secretary. She'd started in a law firm on the twenty-eighth floor, and had then moved to the thirty-third floor, and finally to the forty-first floor, and each time she'd moved it had seemed to me that she was rising higher, both literally and figuratively.

"No," she'd tell me, "I'm only rising literally."

She'd brought me with her to her office once, as part of "Take Our Daughters to Work." I was a boy, but the pedagogical benefits remained applicable. This was when I was six years old or maybe I was seven. We rode an elevator that went as fast as a train, skipping the first thirtysomething floors, and when the doors opened I could see the entirety of Denver. There was Mile High Stadium, there was Coors Field, there were ten thousand people crawling along the sidewalk. I'd spent the day helping my mother open mail, that kind of thing, but mostly I sat in a swivel chair beside her, swinging my legs and watching her type. I was mesmerized by her fingers. She could have been playing a piano sonata at the concert hall, which could also be seen from the window. When it was time for us to go home, her boss came out to meet me, a big bald man in a pin-striped suit, shaking my hand and asking the standard question: what was it I want to be when I grow up, "Now that you've seen the inner workings of a law firm."

Obviously, the correct answer was lawyer.

"I want to be a secretary," I'd told him.

By the fourth green light, there's a woman in the crowd saying to the production assistant, "This is complete bullshit." I realize it's the same woman from the day before, the one with the brown eyes and the sunburned face, whose way I couldn't get out of at the bookstore. This isn't all that coincidental, of course, seeing the same person twice in a town of seven thousand. It's not clear to me if the woman is suggesting that having to wait to cross the street is bullshit or having to wait to cross the street *because of Shaun White* is bullshit. Either way, it's not the kind of talk you hear in Aspen.

"I just do what they tell me," the production assistant says, which apparently is his go-to for all interactions with the public.

But the woman is not persuaded. "That's no excuse," she says.

The production assistant is staring ahead, unperturbed, and the woman is staring at him, perturbed, and I'm staring at her. She's dressed again for an office job in a skirt and heels, and her face appears to have become even more sunburned—or maybe she's just pissed off.

"He's just doing his job, honey," one of the bystanders is explaining to her, as if explaining this will settle the matter, and another tourist is saying that he can see Shaun White coming down the mountain on his snowboard, look, look, look, and everyone is pushing and pulling to look, and I'm pushing the other way, through the crowd, which has doubled in size. "Are you a prompt person?" the owner had asked me at my job interview. "Yes, I am!" I'd said with too-over-the-top conviction. I was doing my best to differentiate myself from the twenty other applicants, which is tough when fielding yes-or-no questions. In the end, it was the father of a friend of a friend who'd put in a good word for me.

"Does Shaun White live in the mountain?" the little girl is asking her mother.

"He will one day," she says.

I know I'm going to be late, and the owner will be covering for me at the front desk, sitting next to the typewriter, gazing into his gallery of unsold art.

The next morning I'm at work, as per usual, one hour already gone by, waiting for something to happen, when the doctor's preface pops straight into my empty head. I can see the word "preface" in all caps, Sans-serif, the words marching across my line of vision, across the paintings, shades and shapes without rhyme or reason, as if the artists gave up. I've been looking at these same paintings since day one on the job. Now, as I'm staring into the vastness of the art gallery, as large and pristine as a high-end hotel lobby without any furniture, an unformed idea is emerging over the horizon of my consciousness. The abstraction of the gallery dovetails with the abstraction of my memory: blotchy, indistinct, non-narrative, yes, childlike. I don't remember the specifics of that afternoon in Denver when I was left with a neighbor. No date, no name, no face. In other words, nothing actionable. I was four or five, maybe I was six, maybe it was winter. I know the doctor would say the memory has intentionally been buried.

Anyway, this is what I'm thinking when the IT guy walks into the art gallery unannounced, lugging his toolkit and his industrial-grade laptop. For some reason he's been hired to come every couple months to update the computer we never use.

"How's it been running?" he wants to know. He's speaking too loudly for what's acceptable, but no one else is here.

"It's running fine," I say.

He seems disappointed. He takes a seat at my desk, peering into the monitor, waking up the computer from deep sleep, clicking around, checking this and that. He's clearly meticulous about his work and I respect this. He's also oblivious to the presence of the typewriter, sitting one foot from his elbow. If he were to lean a little more to the side, he'd hit the carriage return and make it ding. I don't have the heart to tell him that this is the technology of choice for the art gallery.

"I can't find anything wrong," he tells me. We're in agreement. Even so, "I'm going to need to reinstall the firmware," he says. "Just to be safe." I know he's trying to pad his time sheet. I respect this, too.

I make a show of checking my watch, considering, mulling, as if I have things to do. I still have eight hours to go.

While we wait for the firmware to reconfigure, the IT guy leans back in the chair, hands behind his head, and says, surprisingly, "I like that painting." He's pointing to a silver painting, all lines and inscrutable marks.

"What do you like about it?" I ask him. I'm trying to be a pleasantly engaging receptionist, who "will be able to provide basic background information," as stated in the job posting.

"It's pretty," the IT guys says. "It's nice." He doesn't know what else to say. "It would look good above my couch." We laugh. He shrugs. He's not concerned with context and history or metaphor and misdirection.

"I've been getting into baroque lately," he says. He's showing off now.

"So have I," I tell him. I'm lying. I'm happy to draw this conversation out as long as I can.

"What do you like about baroque?" I ask.

"I like his use of color," the IT guy says.

"*His?*"

"Yes."

I wonder if he means Georges *Braque*. Or if he could care less about art and is just trying to ingratiate himself to me, big man at the front desk. For all I know he tells the bookstore person that he likes books, and the florist that he likes flowers. I'm just the receptionist, I want to say to him. I can't do anything for you except sign your time sheet.

He looks around the gallery, elbows on the desk. "Do you have any Baroque?"

"No, we don't."

"You should get some."

"I'll tell the owner."

And the next thing I know I'm giving the IT guy a personal tour of the gallery, a brief introduction to thirty-four works of abstract expressionism before the firmware can finish installing. We go from painting to painting, stopping so I can point out some of the details up close, explain the background of the painter, the significance of the brushstroke, the things you would never be able to see just by looking, the things that you have to know are there in order to be able to see them. I speak like an expert in the field.

We arrive at the silver painting that he likes, and he stops and squints hard, an inch from the canvas, as if he's about to discover something, something figurative maybe, the way we do when we lie on our backs beneath a passing cloud.

"What is it that you're seeing?" I ask him.

He leans back. He leans close. "I'm not seeing anything," he says.

"I'm not, either," I say.

The owner needs me to stay in the art gallery all day the next day, from nine to six, no outdoor Aspen break, so that I can type up the same letter to sixty different collectors about *Untitled X.*

"Lunch is on me," he says, which is fair.

"Dear _____:" each letter begins. "I believe I have something in which you might be interested . . ." It's the same letter as before: provenance, importance, five-figure price. I would be done in an hour if I was allowed to use the computer.

Today the gallery is filled with the sound of metal on metal, as if I'm laboring in a blacksmith's forge, physical exertion necessary for the fabrication of every letter, space, and punctuation mark, including ":". Nothing comes easy in clerical work. If the art gallery wasn't air-conditioned, I'd be wiping my brow. The only pause in the pounding comes when the carriage bell dings to indicate that the edge of the page draws near. This is where the margins can become problematic.

Maybe it wasn't nepotism that got me hired over those twenty other applicants, most of whom came equipped with art history degrees. Maybe it was my ability to type seventy words a minute. This, thanks to my mother, but also thanks to my eleventh-grade typing teacher, who was earnest and exacting, who would spend five minutes before each class expounding to a room of mostly disinterested sixteen-year-olds on how we were developing a skill that would serve us in the real world. Hers was a strictly practical approach to education. "Never mind literature," she'd tell us. "Never mind history." She didn't need to convince me about the efficacy of typing. I'd been made a believer on the forty-first floor overlooking those streets of Denver. I was getting Bs in those other subjects, anyway.

Standing in front of the classroom, she would call out the keys of the home row, that row of gibberish without which communication would not be possible. "A, s, d, f, j, k, l, semicolon!" She was a small woman but her voice boomed over the din of twenty-five typewriters banging out an uneven rhythm. Again and again we students marched, back and forth across the keyboard, a room full of eleventh graders being drilled for a vocational army.

"A, s, d, f, j, k, l, semicolon!"

There was a soothing quality for me in the mind-numbing repetitiveness of *a, s, d, f.*

"If you can master this," the teacher would shout, "you can master anything!"

She knew what she was talking about. One month into the semester, we'd advanced to a complete sentence, "Now is the time for all good men to come to the aid of their country!" she would scream out, and as she screamed, so did we type. "Now is the time for all good men to come to the aid of their country!"

We were never supposed to look at our fingers on the keys, we were never supposed to look at the paper in the carriage, we were only supposed to rely on *muscle memory.*

"A body never forgets," she promised us.

It's past noon when I take a break, my fingertips burning, and order my free lunch from the organically farmed restaurant down the street. I over-order: sandwich, soup, side, soda, side. Might as well. They tell me it'll be here in ten minutes. They sound like they're all smiles. Fifteen minutes later it hasn't arrived. Twenty minutes later I'm starving and I'm not going to tip. This is when the door to the gallery swings open, but instead of the delivery guy walking in, it's the woman from the other day, the one at the funicular who told the production assistant it was "bullshit." She's dressed again in a skirt and heels, and when her heels click on the gallery floor they make a sound that echoes. She stands at my front desk, arms crossed, face still sunburned, eyes still brown, and she says to me, using a voice appropriate for a high-end art gallery with a librarylike atmosphere, almost a whisper, "I'm interested in *Untitled X*."

It turns out her name is Mimi and she's the owner's daughter. In a small town, even this would be considered coincidental. She also happens to work at a hot-shit art gallery on the other side of Aspen. "'Art' runs in the family," she tells me. She puts "art" in air quotes. She's not the front desk receptionist, she's the director. She's two removed from power. "Nepotism," she says. She's jaded. Her father only mentioned her art gallery once, and that was to say, "We're interested in different things." I took that to mean that the other gallery made money.

The first time Mimi takes me there is after hours, for what may or may not be a first date. She has the key to the front door, and when she flicks the overhead lights I'm surrounded by the exceedingly pleasant view of realism, pastoralism, Aspenism. Here are paintings, heavy on the impasto, that are intended to calm the soul, soothe the mind, that would look good hanging above the IT guy's couch. Snow-covered cottages, moonlit villages, lingering dusks, scenes that don't need interpretation or context to make themselves understood. These paintings aren't speaking to the postwar upheaval of the twentieth century, by way of a newly invented visual language. In fact, they're not speaking to anything at all. This is the art of the here and now, made five, ten, fifteen years ago, art that goes for three figures, sometimes four, never five. The gallery does a brisk business at the low end.

As I look at the paintings with Mimi, she doesn't bother asking me, What is it that you're seeing? I can see what it is I'm seeing: a sailboat floating on a lake at twilight, ripples in the water, the moon in the sky, entitled *Sailboat on a Lake at Twilight.*

I'm standing close to Mimi. "Beautiful," I say.

But Mimi gives a wide sweep of her hand, encompassing all the artwork, saying, "I think it's bullshit."

Later, I give myself a tour of the front desk, swiveling in the receptionist's chair, opening and closing the drawers, wondering what it's like to sit here nine hours a day, five days a week, less one hour for lunch.

"Where's the typewriter?" I ask Mimi, which is a joke. We have a good laugh. We have a glass of wine. "Have as much as you want," Mimi says. There's an entire case in the back office, recent year, leftover from the last opening, attended, incidentally, by the living local artist and three hundred people.

"I'm responsible for bartending," Mimi says. "It's in the job description." We have a good laugh about this, too. I imagine eighty bottles of white wine being popped and poured by Mimi, concealing her contempt for the art, for the patrons. "If I get them drunk, they buy more."

The only living artist who ever visited my gallery was an elderly woman, walking with a cane and a caretaker, and whom the owner spoke to in reverential tones. She'd flown from New York to Aspen, two-hour layover in Denver, to spend a couple hours looking at her paintings on the walls. She seemed to like what the owner had done with her work, how it was framed and hung and lit. She'd stood in front of each piece for several minutes, about to say something, but saying nothing. Finally, she asked if anything had sold. "Not yet," the owner had said. He'd sounded hopeful, as if any minute things would change. After she was gone, the owner told me, "She knew Jackson Pollock."

The wine is going to my head, and the swivel chair seems to be swiveling on its own. The gallery is peaceful, innocent, tranquil. Pastoralism come to life.

"Dreamy," Mimi says.

"Yes," I coo.

But she's talking about her father and his art. "He lives in the past," she says. It's hard to argue that.

"Don't we all?" I say.

"I don't," she says. According to Mimi, her father has been trying to unload *Untitled X* for years. "Don't get your hopes up," she tells me.

"I won't," I say.

She thinks her father will eventually go out of business, liquidate the art, bring a merciful end to abstract expressionism in Aspen. I wish I'd known this before taking the job.

"It's tragic," she says.

"Yes, it is," I say, but what I'm imagining is being unemployed in Aspen, walking the streets, trying to find work somewhere, maybe running the funicular.

Mimi tells me that her first love was the Denver Art Museum. Her first love was my day job. Her father would take her there when she was a girl, driving three hours one way for each new exhibit, slowing down to ten miles an hour at the Continental Divide so his daughter could experience the precise moment of before and after in America. She tells me how she would wander through the galleries of the museum alone, looking at the art by herself, understanding it intuitively, immediately, without instruction or guidance. "Art runs in the family," she says. Here she does not use air quotes.

"What was it like working in the café?" she wants to know.

"I stole things," I tell her. I tell her how I would take bags of chips printed with Van Gogh's face and then sell them to the museum guards at half price. I tell it like it's a funny story, but when I'm done she says, "That's sad."

"I thought it was funny," I say.

"We should go there sometime," she says. I'm not sure if she's asking me out on a second date.

"Sure," I say, but I have no interest in going back to Denver.

She tells me when she first discovered one of Monet's water lily paintings, second floor of the museum, she sat in front of it for half an hour. "I was six years old," she says, "maybe I was seven." She remembers with clarity having been transfixed by the great artist's brushwork, the colors, the perspective. Without knowing anything about him, she'd somehow understood that it had been painted by a man with failing eyesight.

"But how could you have known that?" I ask.

She pours me more wine. She pours herself more wine. She turns on the computer and the screen lights up. "Show me how you type," she says.

"I'm driving drunk," I say.

This she finds funny. She's standing close to me. Her hip by my shoulder.

"What should I type?" I ask.

"I don't care," she says.

Before I can conjure something clever, my fingers are moving on their own over the space-age keyboard, seventy, eighty, ninety words a minute, as if I'm skating on ice, no missteps, no typos. "Now is the time for all good men to come to the aid of their country!"

Then Mimi's sitting on my lap, making the first move, making the swivel chair swivel, and when she kisses me, her hair falls in my face, and I can smell the white wine on her breath. The gallery is subsumed by that silence with which I've grown so familiar, and when she comes up for air, she's staring into my eyes, staring hard, a few inches from my face, as if she's just noticed something, astute observer that she is.

"What is it that you're seeing?" I ask.

FAIRGROUND

've only been to one hanging in my life and that was when I was six or seven years old, or maybe I was eight, but who can really remember that far back with complete accuracy? This also happened to be during the period when the city was being rezoned, Sector A now Sector G, Sector G now Sectors Q *and* R, and so on, thanks to the mayor who'd won by a landslide. It was going to take a while for everyone to get used to the changes, but everyone agreed that it would be worth it in the end. Sometimes, when I was out walking with my mom, we would pass a row of school buses lined up like ducks at the crosswalk, waiting

for the light to turn green, the faces of the secured populations looking through the windows with indifference and
resignation, as if they'd been traveling for weeks across the
country rather than hours across the city. They would be
crammed into the buses, children, too, twice as many as the
bus could comfortably hold, their belongings piled on their
laps, often higher than their heads, suitcases, backpacks,
lamps without lampshades. If you could carry it, you could
bring it. That was the directive. That seemed fair.

"Don't stare," my mother would say. "It's not polite."

What I do remember for sure is that I'd been taken to
the hanging as something of an afternoon diversion by
Mr. Montgomery, my stepfather, the first stepfather in a
sequence of several, and with full consent of my mother,
who considered the outing a good opportunity for me to
bond with a man I'd just met a few weeks earlier. "You'll
learn to love him," she'd told me, an upbeat prediction that
as far as I could see was based on little evidence.

The day trip with Mr. Montgomery had also been a
way for my mother to have some alone time so she could
study for her upcoming exam, because this also happened
to be during that period when she'd gone back to school,
mid-thirties, trying to do something different with her life,
something "meaningful," and become a librarian. If all
went well, she'd soon be able to get us out of our apartment
above the nail salon, where we'd been living for a year, and
where the scent of nail polish would waft up through the

vents between the hours of ten and six. I thought it smelled nice, and my mother thought it smelled annoying, and eventually we were so used to it that we no longer smelled it at all. She told me that she'd take me downstairs "one of these days" so that I could have my nails painted at half price—half price being one of the perks of living above a nail salon.

"Think about what color you want," she'd said.

"What colors do they have?"

"They have every color."

"Then I want blue."

"You have to dream bigger than that," she said. She listed colors I hadn't known were colors: orange cream dream, tiger blossom, tickle my heart, timberline violet.

"Tiger blossom," I said.

"Good choice," she said.

Seeing Mr. Montgomery and me off on that fall afternoon, she'd stood in the doorway of our apartment, Dewey Decimal study guide under her arm, telling us, "Have fun, boys!"

"Oh, we will!" Mr. Montgomery had said.

But the prospect of an outing with me had apparently made Mr. Montgomery contemplative, unexpectedly so, and he'd sat in the parked car for a while, saying nothing, hands on the wheel, key in the ignition, motor off, gazing through the windshield at I knew not what. I'd sat there, too, wondering if we were having car trouble. Finally, he'd turned to me, eyes moist, saying how it had just occurred to him, right then, how he was passing the tradition downward. "Do you know what I'm talking about, son?" he'd asked. No, I didn't. "Yes, I do," I said. He seemed moved by this. He rubbed the back of my neck with something like fondness. The sensation was unfamiliar but pleasant. According to Mr. Montgomery, when he'd been a boy about my age, six, seven, or eight, he'd been taken to his very first execution by his father, as had his father before him, and so on down the generational line, great-great-great-grand. I was dubious that Mr. Montgomery had ever been a boy my age, let alone a boy at all, but he appeared to remember the past with emotion. "Like yesterday," he told me. He wiped his eyes with the back of his hand. The back of his hand looked old. This was what fathers did with sons, he said. This was what I would one day do with my sons. He spoke with confidence and assertion.

"I understand, Mr. Montgomery," I said.

"You don't have to call me 'Mr. Montgomery,'" he said.

"I won't," I said.

He wanted me to call him by his first name, William, or one of the variations thereof. "You can call me Will or Willy," he said. "You can call me Bill or Billy."

It was an hour to the fairground and the reminiscences were going to make us late. He leaned forward in his seat as if doing so made the car go faster. Through the windshield the scenery of the city passed by at an alarming rate, occasionally broken by a flash of white space where trees and grass had been eliminated, and where we could briefly glimpse the towering snowcapped mountain, beyond which lay the next city.

Frankly, I didn't know what my mother saw in Mr. Montgomery. They seemed to have nothing in common, beginning with the fact that Mr. Montgomery's primary experience in a public library had been to use the public bathroom. "I needed to pee bad," he'd said. I didn't find this funny, but he and my mother sure did, and they told the anecdote jointly and often, interpreting the distance that separated them on the compatibility index as something that strengthened their bond, rather than a troubling indicator that they were wrong for each other.

Still, the first time I'd met Mr. Montgomery had been for dinner at Applebee's, which had been a promising start. I'd worn slacks and my mother had worn lipstick. They'd sat side by side in the big burgundy booth, and I'd sat across from them, as if they were interviewing me for a job, everyone's hands folded politely on the table. Mr. Montgomery had told me that I could order anything I wanted off the menu, and this added to the air of promise. "Sky's the limit," he'd said. He was showing off for my mother. "He's going to learn to love you," my mother had said to him. I knew he was trying to curry favor with me. I knew he knew I was the lone obstacle for him being able to sleep with my mother.

So I ordered the most expensive thing off the menu, why not, the double-glazed baby back ribs, which I'd never heard of before.

Apparently this was the wrong choice.

"Don't be presumptuous," my mother said.

"How about the mac and cheese?" Mr. Montgomery said. He was referring me to the children's menu.

So I acquiesced and ordered the typical child's fare, chicken fingers and french fries.

"Why not get a milkshake to go with that?" Mr. Montgomery said, trying to prove that he was actually easygoing with money.

"Yummy," my mother said.

"No," I said.

We arrived at the fairground with barely time to spare. The parking lot was filled to capacity and people were streaming through the big white gate, above which read SECTOR N WELCOMES YOU TO THE CITY FAIRGROUND. Soon this would have to be changed to SECTOR V. Mr. Montgomery drove around looking for an empty spot, cursing, going in circles, apologizing for cursing, talking philosophically about how this was everyone else's fault, that this was what happened when you stopped paying attention, big crowds, little sensitivity, no parking. Everything is connected, son, he said. Yes, he was happy that the turnout was good, because good turnout meant there was civic pride. "But civic pride comes at a cost," he said. "Back in my day . . ." he said. He extemporized about the past. I said nothing. "Do you know what I'm talking about?" he said. He didn't wait for an answer. Suddenly he turned to me. "There's going to be blood today, son," he said, as if he were only now realizing what this excursion was all about. "Are you okay with blood?" he asked. He sounded concerned. He sounded as if he were prepared to turn the car around if I had answered no.

I wanted to be okay with blood. But I wasn't so sure. I still had scabs on my knees from a few weeks earlier when my mother had tried to teach me how to ride a bicycle, and just when I was getting the hang of it, I'd crashed into the sidewalk. My mother had comforted me briefly, sweetly, cradling me in her lap, and two women from the nail salon had come over, wearing aprons, smelling of polish. "You have to get right back on, honey," they'd said.

"I like blood, sir," I told Mr. Montgomery,

He liked that I liked blood. "Good boy," he said. He said, "You don't have to call me 'sir.'"

We found a parking spot way on the other side, and when we got to the front gate, Mr. Montgomery paid ten dollars for two tickets on steel bleachers in the hot sun with people sitting in front of us wearing hats so I couldn't see. We'd forgotten our own hats or had not known to bring hats. We were far from the stage but close to the sun. Five minutes in, my forehead was baking and so were the backs of my thighs, but I said nothing because I knew I should not be the kind of boy who complains and orders the most expensive thing off the menu.

"Are you having fun yet?" Mr. Montgomery asked.

"I sure am," I said.

But there was no indication of fun or even the prospect of fun. We were in a venue used for high school football games, and a banner hung breezeless in the air, celebrating a championship from twenty years ago. Next to the banner was a portrait of the mayor, appearing magnanimous and forward-thinking. He'd won by promising that he could do what needed to be done to remedy the persistent problems of the city: plumbing, mail delivery, etc. Also the secured populations. No one could argue that these were problems. No one as yet had been able to figure out how to fix them.

Between the spectators' hats I could glimpse the gallows, fourteen feet off the ground, accessed by a wooden staircase. A rope dangled from the crossbeam, and I knew that this was the instrument of death, but it seemed languid and ineffectual. How this contraption could take a life, much less draw blood, I couldn't understand. Mr. Montgomery told me how in his day they didn't have hangings, but shot the condemned instead. In his father's day, they were beheaded with silver sabers, and so on down the line: guns, swords, poison, fire, great-great-great-grand. He waited for my reaction.

"Wow," I said.

"Times change, son," he said.

Then he bought me popcorn, jumbo-sized, because he was apparently easygoing with money after all, and we both munched on it while waiting for something, anything, to happen, the heat closing in on us, the popcorn falling around our feet.

Mr. Montgomery took advantage of the downtime to muse aloud about his ambitions and intentions for life, life in general, *his* life specifically, which, according to him, had been spent pursuing "objectives," but for reasons that were out of his control had never been "realized." He spoke of life not as a thing to be lived, but *attained*. He used phrases that sounded as if they had been gleaned from my mother's career guidance manuals. He'd been sent to prison for a crime he had not committed but did not want to name. "You're too young, son," he said. It was extortion or fraud. Maybe assault or murder. Whatever it was, he'd done fifteen years. I had pieced it together from late-night conversations overheard through my bedroom door. Here was another thing that my mother had found amusing about his past.

"What was jail like?" I asked him.

"It wasn't jail," he said, "it was prison."

He told me how his business plans had fallen through. He had had investment plans that had fallen through, too.

He had had merger and acquisition plans. Everything had fallen through.

"I try and I try," he said. Despite the odds, he tried. The odds were high and they were stacked against him—him and me. We were in this together. I liked being in something together with someone, but the thought of the odds being against me was troubling.

"You'll find out for yourself one day," he said.

In the hot sun, on the hard bench, with the popcorn running low, Mr. Montgomery marched forward carrying the trajectory of his life without much modulation in his voice. He sounded less like he was conversing and more like he was reciting. There was a very good possibility that he had said all this before, exactly the same way, to other little boys of other pretty mothers. He sat with his elbows on his knees, staring ahead at the hats. "When I dream," he said, "I dream big." He seemed to view dreaming as an achievement in and of itself. He saw the size of his failures as an indication of the size of his dreams. Dream small, fail small. But he was going to turn things around now that he had my mother in his life, and, of course, me. "The ship is changing course," he said. We were lucky charms to him. He rubbed my head as a joke, which I liked. He had an idea for a patent, but he couldn't tell me what it was yet. "I don't want to get too far ahead of myself," he said. It was almost a certainty that he was going to be buying a house for us.

"Would you like that, son?" Sure, I would like that.

I wanted to believe that what he was telling me was the truth, but I think I knew that it was just talk, that it would come to nothing, that his relationship with my mother would come to nothing, that my mother had gotten involved with a dud, which might have said as much about my mother as it did about Mr. Montgomery, and that in six months or so she'd be in her pajamas crying in the living room, post-breakup, berating herself—"I did it again! I did it again!"—and I'd be sitting by her side trying to console her. "No," I'd tell her, "you didn't do it again!" But she had.

And then Mr. Montgomery and I were brought out of our intimate exchange by the sound of chimes coming over the PA system, slow, low, and steady. The fairground fell silent and Mr. Montgomery and I stopped chewing—now was not the time for concessions. Now was the time to stand on the precipice of the profound, which was arriving by way of a procession of thirty officials, their long flowing white robes dragging through the dust of the fairground, their feet in sync with the chimes. The officials ascended the stage, standing side by side, staring out at us, as if they were a graduating class. There was a smattering of polite applause from the spectators, which the officials seemed to appreciate, but the applause was premature, possibly sarcastic, prompted mainly by the fact that there was finally some action occurring, and it died out. The silence resumed. The autumn sun was at its brightest.

"It's the witching hour, son," Mr. Montgomery said.

From within the group of adjudicators appeared the condemned, dressed in a black robe, with a big white beard
that stood in contrast to the black robe, and a beleaguered
face beneath the beard, made sallow by lack of food or sunshine, which contrasted to the murmurs of elation rever-
berating through the stands. The chimes reached twelve
and were replaced by the sound of trumpets, martial, asser-
tive, and prerecorded. The condemned seemed forlorn and
bewildered as he made his way to the front of the stage.
He moved with melancholy steps. He moved alone. He
stopped and faced the audience, prepared to say his last
words, which would do him no good, but which were his
by right. He smiled briefly, unctuously, maybe in the hope
that the thousands in attendance might advocate for him in
this, his final hour, or, at the very least, find him appealing.

"Do they feed him?" I asked Mr. Montgomery.

"Don't feel sorry for him, son," Mr. Montgomery said.
"That's the reason the city is in this mess today.

"What's he done?" I asked.

"Something bad," he said.

The man was from one of the secure populations and
there would be no mercy on him, unless, of course, this
happened to be one of those rare and disappointing occasions when clemency was bestowed by official decree at the
last second. But the chances of that happening were one in a
million, and would be issued by the mayor who'd pondered

it, slept on it, and then appeared on a horse, galloping in, waving the pardon in his hand, demonstrating that regardless of the crime, the populace still maintained a healthy capacity for forgiveness and redemption. *No refunds*, read the fine print on the ticket stub.

The condemned mumbled something into the microphone, barely audible and drowned out by the trumpets. "Louder," people screamed, because no one wanted to miss a word after having waited so long. The screaming unnerved the prisoner and he gawked at the audience, blinking, shrugging, as if to say, *What can I do? I am just one man, I am just one man alone on a stage in this vast arena.* Somewhere a technician flicked a switch and the condemned's voice echoed over the fairground, midsentence, bouncing off the wooden bleachers. "Thank you all for coming today," he said.

It turned out that I had confused the players of the game, and this man, dressed in black, was not the condemned at all, but was a low-level administrator who was here to make the official statement regarding the city's due diligence, etc. "This is the boring part," Mr. Montgomery told me. The boring part was not the same as the waiting part, but it unraveled just as slowly with its list of bylaws and ordinances. Once again, the crowd grew restless. I wanted to rest my head on Mr. Montgomery's shoulder but I wasn't sure if we had reached that point yet in our relationship.

The sun beat down on my face. "Section seven," the man on stage said, "article two . . ." He enunciated everything. This was his moment to shine and he was going to take as long as it took. "Amendment five hundred, chapter twenty," someone in the crowd yelled with mock formality. The line got a good laugh, and it broke the tedium, and the audience went back and forth like that—"Section one thousand, paragraph one million"—trying to outdo each other with clauses and subsections, forcing the administrator to raise his voice, which in turn caused the spectators to frolic more, and it was in the midst of this wordplay that, without any prologue, the thrilling part began.

"Here we go, son," Mr. Montgomery said. He squeezed my elbow.

Half a dozen adjudicators climbed the stairs to the gallows, giving us a glimpse of their loafers beneath their gowns. They surrounded the empty noose, as if the noose were the thing they had come to see. Once again my view was blocked by the patrons in front of me, who were now standing and shouting. Everyone was standing and shouting. "Sit down!" someone yelled from behind. "This is what you get for ten dollars," Mr. Montgomery said to me. I stood on my seat and then I stood on my tiptoes and then Mr. Montgomery did something wonderful and unexpected, lifting me onto his shoulders with one swift gesture, and blocking the view of those behind me without apology.

I wrapped my hands around his chin. His chin was rough and unshaved. The top of his head was thinning.

"Where is he?" I asked.

"Right in front of you," Mr. Montgomery said.

And sure enough, there he was, already standing on the gallows in the middle of all the commotion, dressed in a purple polka-dot uniform with SECURED POPULATION printed on his chest. He looked handsome. He looked glamorous. If they fed him, they fed him well. If he was despondent, he did not appear so. He looked like a movie star dressed as a purple clown pretending to be the condemned, and those who bustled around were the production crew, the hangers-on, fawning over him the way the crew fawn over the leading man. But these hangers-on were having trouble getting the noose over the condemned's head, and each one had to take a turn trying to either loosen or tighten the knot, trying to get the opening wider. They were confused and inept. "Get on with it!" the crowd called, but the truth was that we had waited too long for this moment and now we wanted it to last. Throughout it all, the condemned appeared calm, even dignified. He stared into the audience, perhaps looking for someone he knew, and for a second I thought he might have looked at me, three hundred rows away.

Then the noose was slipped past the man's curls and tightened around his neck, and he stood there as if he were waiting to be lifted up into the air on an amusement park ride, rather than being dropped downward, which was precisely what happened. He was gone in an instant, falling through the trapdoor. Not even a final wave farewell. A gasp from the crowd alerted me to the fact that this was the moment we had come to see. He disappeared alive, and reappeared dead, bouncing and dangling, his feet a few inches above the dusty fairground. If he'd been any taller, he would have landed on the soles of his shoes.

"Wowee!" Mr. Montgomery said. He clapped his hands.

The condemned's body twitched and lurched, and then swung gently to and fro. It all seemed a bit underwhelming. It was like a magic trick that had been bumbled too many times by a novice magician. Even so, we cheered.

The body was still swinging as we filed out of the fairground and into the parking lot. It took Mr. Montgomery a while to get back on the road, what with the thousands of cars and all, lots of honking in celebration, trying to sustain the communal feeling for as long as possible. Mr. Montgomery let me honk a few times for fun. By the time we were heading home, the sun had begun to set, casting a poetic pink light over the snowcapped mountain in the distance, beyond which lay the other city. We were quiet for a while, Mr. Montgomery and I, and then I was sleepy. Mr. Montgomery rubbed the back of my neck with affection.

"Where was the blood?" I suddenly thought to ask him.

"That was just a figure of speech," Mr. Montgomery said.

This was strangely disappointing for me, which is what I was thinking right before I fell asleep, my head on Mr. Montgomery's lap.

Just as it would later be disappointing for my mother, who had also taken Mr. Montgomery at his word when he assured us that he would help facilitate some sort of change in our lives. But six months later, nothing had happened, and my mother had reached her limit, and was throwing Mr. Montgomery out of the apartment. "I want you out of here," she told him one night, as I watched from my bedroom door. "And *that's* not a figure of speech!" In order to emphasize her point, she threw a teacup at him. She'd meant to maim but had missed her mark, and the cup had hit the wall, surprisingly staying intact, rolling like a ball, and coming to rest in a corner by the couch by the window with the drapes wide open so that we could see out and the neighbors could see in and we could see the glow cast from the neon lights of the nail salon.

Mr. Montgomery was smiling, as if the whole episode might be comic, like going to the public library to use the public bathroom was comic. His smile made him look enfeebled and emasculated. He mustered a reasonable, "This is *our* home." He sounded so imploring that I knew he didn't stand a chance in this debate.

When I woke the next morning, he was in the living room, packing up his belongings in four empty cardboard boxes that he'd gotten off a loading dock at the grocery store. MARSHMALLOW WHIP, the boxes read. MAYONNAISE. *Three-quart containers times twelve.* Boxes meant for food were now being filled with clothes and mementos of the bittersweet past. He told me to be good, son, to take care of myself. Considering the way it was ending, it seemed a wise decision that I'd never gotten beyond referring to him as "sir."

He was teary-eyed when he rubbed my head goodbye, in the same manner that he'd rubbed it when he'd told me that I was his good luck charm. So much for good luck. I was hoping he might give me a few dollars so I could have some spending money, but there was no way of asking for this without seeming opportunistic. Watching him gather his things, I saw that there was something of the condemned about him, being summoned to his own personal gallows, which in this case was the outside world, with my mother as the hangman, I as the passive specta-tor. As he was exiting through the front door, holding the last of the cardboard boxes, he stopped and stared back at me, his face despondent, his posture defeated. Then he put the box down and reached into his pocket, rustled around, and handed me five dollars. "Invest that wisely," he said.

What I invested it in was my very first manicure at the nail salon, half price, where I chose tiger blossom, like I said I would, and my mother picked something called pink smoothie. We sat side by side, just the two of us, which is how I liked it.

"Your hands are so soft!" the technician kept saying to me.

"Thank you," I said.

Through the window I could see the neon sign blinking WALK-INS WELCOME, but the letters were of course backward.

METAPHOR OF THE FALLING CAT

It was about a year after the car accident when the thoughts came back to me. They'd been gone so long that I'd forgotten all about them, but when they came back, they came back fast. They came back all at once.

I was at my get-well party when it happened. "Just for you," my brother had said, putting his arm around my shoulder, breathing in my face. There was a big sign on the wall that said, GET WELL SOON, WALLY, but I'd been well for four months. We all knew the party was really just for my brother, just so he could show off his wife's newfound culinary skills, and show off his Brooklyn brownstone, which he'd remodeled from scratch, all cherrywood and spiral staircase. There were fifty people milling around, chatting with their mouths full of shrimp. Most of them I'd never seen before. I wanted to make a statement by not eating anything, but after fifteen minutes I gave in and loaded up my plastic plate.

"Good, right?" one of my in-laws said.

He was right, it was good.

Up and down the spiral staircase my mother and father flitted, praising everything they saw, followed by aunts and uncles, cousins of cousins, family I hadn't heard from in years, probably wouldn't hear from again in years. "We were so worried about you," they said as they passed, but none of them had come to visit me in the hospital.

Everyone was dressed casually for the occasion, flip-flops and tank tops, but I was wearing a tie, because there was a chance I might meet someone who might do something for me. "Something" meant anything other than driving a dairy truck for the city, which is what I'd been doing for two years, six days a week, before an SUV swerved into my lane at eighty-five miles an hour, at five o'clock in the morning, sending myself and four thousand eggs through the windshield. I'd broken both legs and injured my spine. Now I was collecting workers' comp, despite having made a full recovery, lying to the doctors about my health, hoping to stretch my checks out until Plan A finally took shape. Plan A was the mystery guest I was going to meet at this party.

Prior to Plan A, however, I had had a very different Plan A. This one dreamed up during that long convalescence in which no one had come to visit me, in which I had nothing but downtime to contemplate my life at twenty-one in a dairy truck, dressed in baby-blue overalls with my name stitched on the breast pocket as if I were a child who might get lost.

I'd made a friend in the hospital, Sylvester Y., middle-aged, with a shattered coccyx, who did mail order from home. It was good money for little work. I was envious of him, and I said so. He had a dead son of whom I reminded him. "Same hair," he told me, "same chuckle." It was unsettling, but I got used to it.

Together, we'd hatched our scheme one morning, six weeks into my stay, the two of us sitting around in our wheelchairs, staring at the wall, waiting for the nurses to come get us.

"So I was watching this episode of *Law & Order* last night . . . ," said Sylvester, who was always watching the original *Law & Order* or one of its spinoffs, and then telling the patients and doctors about it as if it were real life and he had really been there and everyone else should have really been there, too.

"You ever do anything except watch TV?" I'd asked him once.

"Yes," he said, "sometimes I look at YouTube."

His intention had been to regale me with the details of this particular *Law & Order* episode, but, lolling there in the fluorescent hallway, with our minds free to wander, we'd begun to take the story apart and reassemble it, bit by bit, from the criminal's perspective, each of us offering our own piece of the puzzle—basement entry, getaway car— until it had come together so perfectly, so naturally, that we didn't know what we were doing until we were done. Afterward, we sat silently, breathing slowly, staring at the wall with the rainbow mural as if at a masterpiece. But now four months had passed with no word from Sylvester, chuckle or no chuckle, and my checks would soon be running out.

Two hours into my party the hors d'oeuvres were starting to get to me. I was perspiring near the bay window while a man in sandals tried to explain how we were related. "Your grandmother's sister and my mother's brother . . ." He had crumbs on his chin. I wanted to get away from him, far away, to get outside to where the children were playing, where the real party was happening. Through the bay window I could hear them shouting invented obscenities inspired by what they'd consumed that afternoon. "Ketchup!" they shouted. "Hamburger!" Their words held secret meaning. They responded with mock outrage. I watched them knock each other down and get back up. Nothing could hurt their young limbs. Nothing could dissuade them. The time for living was *now*.

For a moment I swayed unsteadily, fearing I might vomit on my relative's exposed toes. He was oblivious, sketching the family tree in the air, four cousins out, three generations down, branches upon branches. I couldn't follow a thing.

"It's all interconnected," he said.

"It sure is," I said, and I pushed past him and fled into the backyard, where a breeze was blowing and dusk was coming.

"Come play with us, Uncle Wally," the children cried, even the ones who weren't my nieces or nephews. I was popular. I was famous. They grabbed me tight around the legs, asking if they could see the injury, asking why I was wearing a tie.

"Are you rich?" they wanted to know.

"I will be," I said.

They were excited by my appearance, and I was revived. They weren't squeamish with blood and scars, so I rolled up my pant leg, just past the calf, right where the steering wheel had cut diagonally across the flesh and severed the bone. "Here and here," I told them, but it was obvious where they needed to look. Their eyes were wide, their faces flushed. They wanted to know if my leg was made of metal, they wanted to know if they could touch. "Of course," I said, and they lined up, taking turns, running their fingers along the twisted curve of my shin. First my niece and nephew examined, then their little friends, then the friends of their friends, then this woman, suddenly, one of the mothers I supposed, wearing a red dress with a yellow sash that accentuated her hips.

"Does it hurt, Wally?" she asked. How she knew my name, I didn't know. I had a brief image of hugging her and kissing her on the lips.

"No," I said, "it doesn't hurt anymore."

"That's good," she said. She was full of empathy and kindness, this woman, with her brown hair and brown eyes, and when she bent down to gently run her fingers along the wound I could glimpse the tops of her breasts.

I said, "Whose mother are you?" And she looked up at me, laughing, and all the children around her were laughing, dancing and laughing at the funny joke I had made, and it was then that I realized, with horror, that this woman wasn't a woman at all, but a little girl, maybe eight years old, maybe six. That's when the thoughts came back to me.

What came back specifically and vividly was the comic book shop in New Jersey that my brother took me to soon after he'd gotten his driver's license. It was forty miles out-side of the city and housed in a converted depository that still said A&J TOMATOES from back when everything was farmland. Light bulbs hung from the rafters, shining bad light on a million-plus comic books stuffed in trunks and bins and whatnot. The owner of the store was an over-weight man, three hundred pounds, who had played college football years ago, but now sat in a wooden booth ten feet off the floor so that he could observe the goings-on in his establishment. Next to him was the cash register, and when you paid your money you had to place it in a little wicker basket that he would lift up on a string. The rumor was that if he caught you shoplifting he'd take you out by the dumpsters and beat you with a baseball bat and then let you keep the merchandise.

No one ever knew what they were going to uncover in this store, what first edition they might find buried under a pile of worthlessness. So the patrons hunted as if they were squirrels, clawing, scraping, until the owner, feeling put-upon, would shout through his bullhorn, "No more looking! Let's make a selection!" His voice would boom through the depository as men and boys obediently fell into line, each one waiting his turn with the little basket on the string.

It took forty-five minutes to get to A&J Tomatoes and my brother used the drive as an opportunity to dispense advice. He was good at advice. He was seventeen and I was twelve. He was going to college and I was getting bad grades. *Study hard* was something he'd suggest. Also, *apply yourself.* "Find something you like," he'd tell me, "and pursue it with everything you have. Like geometry." I was terrible at geometry, but his counsel made sense in theory, and midway through the trip I would see inner passion materializing, and also dedication, and all the loose ends of my life tying up in a bow. "I'm going to do it this time!" I'd say, pounding my fists on my knees, and my brother would put his hand on my shoulder, lovingly, saying, "I know you can, Wally." But we both knew that it was most likely hopeless, that he was saying the things that my father had stopped staying a long time ago because my father had given up.

My brother owned five thousand comic books, sealed in individual plastic sleeves, organized alphabetically and chronologically, and stored upright on shelves in the utility closet so that their spines wouldn't become creased and diminish their value. He was keen on keeping them in pristine condition so that they would "last forever." But eventually he outgrew them and went to college, and the collection he gave to me as a farewell gift. The day he left, I stood in our lobby on Eighty-Third Street with Mom and Dad, watching him drive off, waving in the rearview. Then the next thing I did was haul the comic books into my bedroom and take them out of their plastic sleeves and stuff them in the bottom of my closet. I didn't care about keeping them pristine, I cared about reading them, each and every one of them. Batman, Spider-Man, Captain America, and all those heroes in between. Heroes who died, heroes who came back, heroes who died and never came back.

I began at the beginning, back when they cost twenty-five cents each, lying in bed at night with a flashlight, slowly making my way toward four dollars. My father would occasionally appear in the doorway, frustrated, sullen, staring at me, saying, "Your brain's going to turn to mush."

I'd say, "It's too late to worry about that now, isn't it?"

He had no answer for that, and by the time I'd finished reading them I was close to graduating from high school myself and driving out to New Jersey alone.

And it was there, at the comic book shop, one afternoon during the summer I turned nineteen, that I saw something that would alter my brain forever.

I remember that it had been a Sunday, and that the store had been more crowded than usual for a Sunday. It had also been hotter than usual, one of the first hot days of the summer, and the only fan in the depository was the fan that blew on the owner in his booth. I'd been in the store for about half an hour, perspiring, trying to push my way through to the more coveted areas, before finally giving up and wandering off to a corner in the back where I found a metal bin that was filled with old issues of *The Incredible Hulk*. A light bulb hung above my head, poorly placed, casting shadows and causing me to twist in order to bring the comic books into the light. It didn't really matter, I'd already read all the issues, but I flipped through them anyway, bored out of my mind, until I came across a magazine about the size of a comic book, but no more than fifteen pages, with a picture of a little girl on the cover.

It wasn't that unusual to discover things in the shop that didn't belong—I'd once found thirty years of the Newark Yellow Pages—and at first glance I didn't think much of anything regarding this particular magazine. Perhaps it was for children, I thought, or *about* children, or about child rearing. But there was something peculiar about the photograph that made me linger a little longer, something about the way the little girl was smiling at the camera, strangely coquettish. She was dressed in a checkered skirt and pink socks that drooped to her ankles. *Lollipop Girls*, the title read in purple typeface. The magazine looked like it had been printed quickly and cheaply, bad ink on thin paper, and I would have put it down if it hadn't been for the outrageous price that caught my eye, surely a typo, printed on the cover: one hundred and thirty-five dollars.

So I bent forward out of the shadows, and I opened the magazine to see that the girl was now without her checkered skirt, sitting on top of her bed, encircled by a dozen teddy bears. She was still smiling at the camera, as if nothing were out of the ordinary, as if she might just be having her school picture taken without her skirt. Her polka-dot underpants were showing. "My name is Sabrina," the caption read. She had long blond hair that was pulled back by a rubber band. Behind her, a window faced out onto what looked like an orchard or a forest. The scene had an idyllic make-believe quality, as if it were from some playland or from Disney. Perhaps this is a Disney story, I told myself. But on the next page the girl's socks were missing, and so was her shirt. Her toenails were painted with girly sparkles, but her chest was like a boy's. She sat with her chin on her palms, her elbows on her knees, her knees slightly parted. She was playing at disinterest. She looked polished and clean, as if she'd just come out of a bath. She seemed to be enjoying the attention of the camera, seemed even to be suppressing laughter in what might all be fun and games. Fun and games that now included a man who sat beside her on her bed. He was dressed and bald. He could have been a professor or a father. He could have been the friendly neighbor next door in the orchard. His enormous body contrasted with her delicate one. A black bar had been printed to obscure his eyes but you could see that he was laughing along with the girl. One of his hands encircled her waist, pulling her closer to him in an easygoing way, as his other hand tugged gently at the elastic band of her polka-dot underpants.

I turned the page.

"No more looking! Let's make a selection!"

I called Sylvester Y. on a Tuesday. "He's not here on Tuesdays," his wife said. He'd never mentioned a wife when we were together in the hospital. He'd only mentioned a son. Where Sylvester was, she did not know. When he would be back, she did not know that, either.

I didn't believe her. What I believed was that he'd taken our beautiful plan and executed it by himself.

"Is he there on Wednesdays?" I asked, but she'd already hung up.

I'd waited too long to call. I understood this. "Be proactive," my brother had always told me when we were growing up. But I was young and didn't know what "proactive" had meant and now it was too late. The dairy bosses no longer cared that I was infirm—which I wasn't. They wanted me back to work. They wanted me back in the truck.

The landlord was on to me, too. Or at least I thought he was. In the morning I would see him outside tinkering on the roof, shirt off, tool belt on. It wasn't even eight o'clock and he'd worked up a sweat. If you didn't know he was the landlord, you would think he was the guy who worked for the landlord. "Good morning," he'd call, and I'd wave back with neighborliness, thinking about how in a month I'd be asking him for a break.

"How are you feeling?" he wanted to know.

"Ups and downs," I said. He seemed dubious.

It took a dozen more calls to Sylvester before he finally called me back. I could hear the television going in the background. "If you're not serious about this," I told him, "tell me now." I was trying to be cool, but then I shouted, "Tell me now!"

He said he was serious, he was damn serious. Apparently, he was in the same position that I was, misleading the authorities, stretching out the benefits. His wife had acted with caution.

"Do I sound like the government?" I said.

"You can never be too careful," he said.

He seemed old on the phone, he seemed like he might be on pain medication, and I felt bad for him. I felt bad for shouting. According to Sylvester it wasn't Sylvester who wasn't serious, but some third party whom he'd never mentioned, who'd decided to drop out at the last minute. It was the third party who had the connection. The connection was the cousin of a friend. It was the friend who had the cousin. It was the cousin who worked at the credit union. It was the credit union we were trying to get to.

But Sylvester Y. said that it was better without this third party because it meant one less person we'd have to split it with.

"Any day now," he said. "Wait for my call."

"I don't believe you," I said.

But I had no choice but to wait, trying to hold everything at bay, waking each morning to the sound of the landlord's hammer tinkering just above my head.

———

A few days after I had discovered that magazine, I went back to the comic book shop. I knew it was a troubling sign that I was going back. I knew it was a troubling sign that I knew it was a troubling sign and that I still couldn't stop myself.

The store hadn't even opened yet when I arrived and I had to stand around with three guys who wanted to talk to me about Batman. The moment the owner unlocked the door I was right back in the corner, pawing through the metal bin with the back issues of *The Incredible Hulk*, the lone light bulb dangling above my head. But the magazine was gone.

On the floor by my feet sat a gigantic trunk filled with third-rate comic books going for half price, *Richie Rich*, that type of thing. I got down on my knees and went through those, too. But the magazine wasn't there. Nor was it in the next three boxes I looked in. Nor was it in any of the crates, chests, or cases. Through the depository I roamed, rummaging, rooting, elbowing my way into all the nooks and crannies. Two hours later, my fingers stained with ink, I returned to where I'd started: the bin with the issues of *The Incredible Hulk*. Surely, I must have thumbed through too heedlessly and overlooked the obvious. But no, the magazine wasn't there. And now that I had begun, I couldn't stop myself from retracing every one of my steps, stooping down to the *Richie Rich* comic books again, where I was certain that someone, the owner maybe, must have seen the magazine and mistaken it for a children's magazine and decided to put it with something more age-appropriate.

Beneath my logic lurked the knowledge that the task before me was tremendous, the odds astronomical. Amid the piles of comic books, stacked floor-to-ceiling, it would never be possible to find something specific. No one ever entered the store thinking they could. They entered to browse and discover, not locate. But the moment the thought of surrender entered my head, it was engulfed by a more powerful thought: the image of the girl. Her pretty face, her blond hair, her coquettish smile. I could picture her clearly. "My name is Sabrina." Her knees parted and her polka-dot underpants slowly being tugged away. If only I could have turned the page to see what had happened next. If only I could have caught one more glimpse of her, I would have been satisfied.

So I went forward with renewed strength and vitality, the girl perfectly formed in my mind, tantalizingly formed, willfully ignoring the owner's command to stop looking and make a selection, until finally, near closing time, hungry and exhausted, my legs weak beneath me, I was overtaken by the terrifying certainty that what I was doing was pointless. The magazine was no longer in the store: it had been *purchased*.

———

Thus began my season of compulsion. I could not rid myself of the images. No matter what I did, the face of the girl remained fixed in my brain. I tried jogging. I tried swimming. I tried working double-shifts in the dairy truck. But every thirty minutes, every fifteen minutes, there she was again, looking at me through the windshield.

"Save me," she called, her voice small and plaintive. But rather than driving a truck down city streets, I was flying through the sky over an orchard. The story unfolded in comic book form with panels and dialogue bubbles, with me plummeting through the air, full of force and vigor, the way superheroes do, my cape billowing, crashing straight through the girl's bedroom window. The man with the black bar across his eyes fell to his knees, begging me not to hurt him. "Please," he implored, "have mercy on me." But the time for mercy had passed. I lifted him by his collar and hurled him through the open window. And then it was just the girl and me, alone in her bedroom, the girl jumping into my arms, thanking me for having rescued her. She was small and light. She felt fragile like a doll. "My name is Sabrina," she said.

Thinking that I might somehow be liberated by destroying the comic books, I drove them to the dump one afternoon, two car trips with the backseat filled, and I tossed them over, all five thousand of them, including first editions.

But still she remained.

In the spring I went to see a psychologist, on West Fourteenth Street, who I only told half the story to.

"Obsession" is what I said I was suffering from, it seemed

an apt enough description, but I never said obsession about *what*.

"Obsession in general," I said.

He agreed with the term, he wanted to "know more." I couldn't give him more. He wanted to know about my childhood, but my childhood had been ordinary. I suggested that perhaps this was causing my obsession: ordinariness.

"Let's not worry about diagnosing," he said. He said it gently, but I wasn't sure what he meant.

Every Thursday at one o'clock I lay on his maroon couch, staring at the ceiling, listening to the air-conditioning blowing, waiting for either of us to start talking.

One afternoon, apropos of nothing, I happened to tell him about a cat I'd once had when I was a little boy, Lucky Joe, who'd fallen sixteen flights off my balcony on East Eighty-Third Street.

"He was a beautiful cat," I said.

"Cats don't just fall off balconies," the therapist said.

But this one had. He'd been perched on the railing, the way cats are wont to do, and he'd been startled by something and lost his footing. I remember that my brother and I went downstairs, both of us sobbing, to retrieve the body, but we could find nothing.

"How could there be no body?" the therapist had wanted to know.

Perhaps I'd remembered it wrong.

"Perhaps you've remembered it right," he said.

"Perhaps he survived," I said.

He was a nice enough man, this therapist, full of patience and understanding, though I often wondered how long the understanding would last if he'd known what was really running through my troubled mind. But the price was two hundred dollars a session, and my insurance only covered forty percent, not counting a deductible, and after four months I cut off the treatment by way of a phone call.

I hoped that after some time passed I would simply forget everything and go back to being who I had been: a young man driving a dairy truck for a living. How quaint that life now seemed. And it was true that the girl's face faded from memory, but it was immediately replaced by the faces of other little girls. Little girls in Times Square, for instance. Or in the playground. Eventually, I forgot if Sabrina had been blond or brunette. Eventually, I forgot her name. I began to stop by the elementary school after my morning shift and watch the girls screaming with glee in their last moments of freedom. Then the bell would ring and they would disappear inside and I would drive home.

I'm just going through a phase, I told myself. But the phase continued into winter. I began to park my truck on side streets, where girls walked alone on their way to school. They would pass by, oblivious to me sitting in the front seat, their books and bags occasionally brushing against the side of the truck. Sometimes I'd roll down my window and rest my baby-blue coverall arm on the door. If a girl approached I would smile at her. It seemed like it would be quite easy to start up a conversation. "What's your favorite class?" for instance. The prospect of such ease enticed me. Then it terrified me. I promised I would never park there again. I broke the promise. So I promised again. Then I broke it again.

Then one morning I went through the windshield at five o'clock in the morning and suddenly I had other things to occupy my mind.

I had other things to occupy my mind now, too. Namely, Sylvester Y. calling me, and not a moment too soon, with good news: the third party was back in. He was back in and ready to go.

"Didn't I tell you?" Sylvester said. He was shouting and laughing.

The old feelings of possibility returned. "Yes," I said, "yes, you did tell me!" My voice quavered with gratitude. How could I have ever doubted? I feared for a moment that I might weep.

We met at his house two nights later, deep in Queens. Our plan was to meet to talk about our plan. That was the first step. After the first step came *action*. After action came new beginnings.

"Come on in, Wally," Sylvester said. He shook my hand like a businessman. I liked that. He lived in one of those small houses, once new, now poor. "I'm glad you could make it," he said. He made it seem as if I'd been the one holding everything up. He was dressed in a sports coat that was too tight for him because he was a big man. He smelled like cologne. He hobbled with affliction.

I was surprised to find his wife waiting in the living room. Was she the third party? She was dressed like she might be on her way out to a show, heels and lipstick.

"This is the one I told you about," Sylvester said to her. She took both my hands in hers. "It's a pleasure to meet you," she said. She held my gaze too long.

The television was on, tuned to the Yankees game, turned up loud. Above the television was the mantel. On the mantel was a portrait of a young man I assumed was their deceased son, captured around the age of ten. Sylvester was right, the boy could have been my younger brother. I wanted to tell them that I was sorry for their loss, but too much time seemed to have passed.

The wife set a plastic bowl of potato chips on the coffee table. "Help yourself," she said. I took a handful and sat down on the couch in the corner. Sylvester switched off the

TV, and the little living room went silent and calm, and then he said, "First things first, I want to thank you for coming today."

I told him, "I wouldn't miss it for the world."

This delighted him and his wife, they smiled and laughed, and the laughter went on for a while. I kept hoping his wife would leave us to it, to get down to business, but instead she sat beside me.

Next to Sylvester was an easel with a giant pad of paper propped on it. He pulled out a blue marker from his pocket and uncorked it with a flourish.

"Thank you for taking time out of your busy schedule," he announced, which made no sense.

"I don't have a schedule," I said.

He ignored this. "I know what it's like to be a working-man." He spoke with a false familiarity, a salesman's tone, as if he were meeting me for the first time. He started sketching a map on the pad. At the top of the map was the credit union I presumed, at the bottom was us, in the middle was the third party. It was a simple pyramid and it made sense. What didn't make sense was that he was talking to me about toilet paper and facial tissue, about how doesn't everyone need these things. He would sell to me, he explained, and I'd sell to others. "Everyone makes money from money," he said.

I leaned forward on the couch. "What exactly are you talking about?" I asked.

Sylvester paused and put the cap on his marker. He affected a sad face. "I knew you'd be skeptical," he said. Then he smiled an overly warm smile. "I was skeptical once, too."

"Skeptical about what?" I asked.

"I'm not skeptical," his wife said.

"What happened to our plan?" I said.

"We've changed our plan," he said.

"This is a *good* plan," his wife said.

"This is a better plan!"

"This is an opportunity!"

"An opportunity for what?" I was standing now.

"Tell him about the opportunities," his wife said.

"I'd be most happy to." He cleared his throat and began: "I buy bulk from my contact and you buy bulk from your contact—which is *me.*"

"This only comes around once-in-a-lifetime," the wife said.

"The gentleman above me," Sylvester continued, "made a hundred and fifty thousand dollars last year." His wife whistled low.

"The gentleman above him made three hundred and thirty-five thousand." He wrote the number on the pad as if writing it would make it so.

"Laundry detergent," the wife said. "Everyone needs laundry detergent."

Sylvester handed me a brochure. "Promise me you'll at least consider it." On the cover was a montage of household products along with a couple reclining on a beach.

"Maybe," I said.

"I sure hope so," Sylvester said.

"I think he will," the wife said.

A BEGINNER'S GUIDE
TO ESTRANGEMENT

've got a thirty-day visa, but I'm only going to be using six of them, and the clock's ticking. It's already taken me fourteen hours to get here to see my dad, starting from JFK, and that's not including the three hours I spent sitting in the Istanbul Airport at five-thirty in the morning or the extended turbulence over the Caspian Sea that made me rest my face on my tray table. Nor does it include the nine months for me to be approved for the visa, because that's a separate journey traversed by way of global bureaucracy. When I do finally land, the airsickness is replaced by the jet lag, which kicks in hard and fast, a toxic combination of depletion, dejection, and befuddlement. The light in the airport is bright like dawn, but the airport's empty like night, and I can't remember if it's technically yesterday or tomorrow or today. I suppose I'd been expecting to arrive into some gray, grim terminal, something sepulchral and seventies, something *Argo*, given the extent of my ignorance and preconceived notions. Instead, the place is tubular and shiny and twenty-first century, and hanging above me is a giant sign that announces, with surprising warmth and conviviality, WELCOME TO IMAM KHOMEINI INTERNATIONAL AIRPORT.

This welcome sign is the lone thing written in English, and this is going to be Impediment #1 toward a more nuanced understanding. Surrounding me on all sides is a language comprised of swishes and dots, more art than alphabet, drawn in cursive with a calligraphic flourish and reading right to left. Lodged somewhere at the bottom of my suitcase is the Lonely Planet Persian phrase book, which I'd purchased next-day delivery from Amazon, back when I was all-in on puncturing the bubble, and which I'd begun studying in earnest in the comfort of my American home until I realized the amount of effort that was required for even minimal proficiency. Now I'm standing underneath the big good-natured sign, trying my best, with jet-lagged fingers, to pop a prepaid SIM card into my iPhone, because my dad told me the first thing I needed to do was let him know when I'd arrived. "Put my mind at ease," he'd said; he was speaking for both of us. I can hear a beeping on the other end of the phone line, ever so faintly, as if a truck is backing down a city street, but whether this beeping is an indication of my dad's phone ringing or a busy signal I have no idea. I keep anticipating that he's going to pick up at any moment and utter the Persian equivalent of "Good morning" or "Good evening," something from chapter one of the Lonely Planet Persian phrase book, followed by a mostly convoluted conversation that will be made worse by his accent, my jet lag, his elderliness, and the uncomfortable truth that we don't really know each other.

With the phone pressed to my ear, I'm aware of a small cluster of government officials about fifty feet away, bearded and dressed in black, sweating despite the twenty-first century air-conditioning, and who are probably wondering what kind of person is in such a rush to make a phone call with a prepaid SIM card. The chance of being suspected makes me feel as if I have something to be suspected *of*, which I do, of course, but only on an emotional level. They resemble actors straight out of central casting, these half dozen sweaty and dark-haired men, *stereotypes* to put it another way, but I know that my perspective is the American perspective, and the central casting I'm referring to is Hollywood's. In other words, the point of view I have is the one I've been conditioned to have.

It's been fifteen years since I last saw my dad. It'd been another fifteen years before that. Now I'm almost thirty-five and he's past sixty-five and there's a good possibility that we don't have another fifteen-year increment to spare. Six months ago I'd received an email from him, out of the blue and in impeccable English, with the subject line "Catching up," as if we corresponded regularly, instead of only on my birthday. "Dear Danush," he began, using my Persian name, which I never use except on official documents, and then without any segue he went into an extended account of how beautiful Iran was in the spring. Mountains, lakes, rivers, mountains. "Perhaps you haven't ever been made aware of this," he wrote. Why, I wondered, would I have been made aware? He continued for another paragraph or so, waxing poetic, showing off his ability to turn a phrase in his second language, while probably also allaying the concerns of the censors, who would have been flattered by such a rhapsodic assessment of their country, as would anyone. There was no "catching up" to be had in any real sense in the email, and by the time I'd reached the end of it, I understood intuitively that what my dad was trying to say, without saying it outright, was, "I would like to see you."

He'd signed it, "Your father," a formal closing, to be sure, and a debatable one, considering he's been my father mostly in biological terms, as opposed to my "real" father, by whom I mean my stepfather, Chip McDade, who's been my father in empirical terms. Chip McDade, who'd moved me and my mom out of our apartment in outer Queens, directly across from a nail salon, Nails Something Something, and all the way up to Upstate, where we lived in a mid-Atlantic colonial with in-ground pool, among other suburban amenities. Chip McDade, who taught me how to throw a football, how to drive a car, and who'd had the foresight to give me his last name, because 9/11 and the Axis of Evil were coming, and why be Danush Jamshid when you can be Danny McDade? "Let the brake out slowly, son," he would say, the car moving herky-jerky through the Walmart parking lot, after hours on an Upstate evening. Chip has always called me "son," and I've always called him "Chip." "Hi, Chip." "'Bye, Chip." "I love you, Chip." When I reference my biological dad, which is seldom, I call him "Dad." This has never failed to cause a flicker of disappointment to appear in Chip's eyes. But by "Chip," I mean my "dad," and by my "dad," I mean "the person I've never really known."

And if my dad thinks Iran is beautiful in the spring, the American government doesn't agree. It thinks the opposite, and it thinks it year-round. Its travel advisory for Iran is, frankly, "do not travel." Strictly speaking, this is categorized as a Level 4 advisory, as per the State Department website, 4 out of 4 levels, i.e., ascension not possible and, depending on a nation's foreign policy, a certain kind of accomplishment in its own right. (As a point of comparison, the Level 3 advisory only gently suggests that you "reconsider travel" for a list of countries that somehow includes Lebanon and the Sudan.) I discovered all of this and more one evening, sitting in front of my computer, trying to figure out how to get a visa, snow falling over the mid-Atlantic colonials. Before me lay the unrelenting reality of not only what *is*, but also what *could have been*, that alternate reality of Danush Jamshid, persona non grata made flesh, if WASP mom had decided to move to Iran, who knows why, circa 1983, height of the Iran-Iraq War, where she would meet and fall in love with Dad, as opposed to the other way around: Dad immigrating to America from Hormozgan Province to study engineering at Long Island University, where he would meet and fall in love with Mom, who was majoring in *English Lit*—already incompatible in terms of career trajectory. "He was handsome and charming," she'd tell me years later, filling in the blanks of my origin story as quickly, and with as many clichés, as she could. As for the other incompatibilities they shared, those would have included religion, culture, politics, and several more blue-chip relationship benchmarks that would have most likely seemed wholly immaterial within the confines of the inaccurate and nonrepresentational world of the college campus. Anyway, that marriage was no longer, sadly, and Danush Jamshid was no longer, thankfully, the last remaining signs of him being the recessive genes of bushy eyebrows and a dark tint to his skin, but the latter only apparent in a certain light. When asked by well-meaning strangers if I'm of Italian or Greek descent, I'll take the easy way out and say yes, great-grandfather on my mom's side or something. No one has yet been able to determine what I'm actually concealing behind the forged last name of McDade, which, during another historical time period in the United States, would have been an ethnic liability of even greater magnitude.

Despite the travel advisory of "do not travel," the State Department web page for Iran still managed to showcase an optimistic, reverential, and contradictory "holiday letter" to the Iranian people, written several years earlier by then–Secretary of State John Kerry and, by the time of my reading it, dated and irrelevant. That it remained prominently displayed on the website was evidence of continued hope for happier days to come between the two nations— or perhaps it was simply governmental neglect and resignation, like the store that's gone out of business but still has its sign up. The letter had been composed back when the experts were positive that things had finally taken a turn for the better with Iran, but now no longer, now progress, now new beginnings, now the cover of *Time* magazine. "This week around the world," Secretary Kerry had written, "Iranians celebrated the festival of Shab-e-Yalda . . ." Add Shab-e-Yalda to the list of things about which I'd never been made aware. Kerry's over-the-top tone extolling the inherent majesty of Iran was similar to what my dad's had been in his email to me, but Kerry was writing primarily with nuclear weapons in mind, not springtime weather, and he had closed by saying that he remained hopeful that both countries would continue to address their differences so that "all our children and grandchildren have the future they deserve." Herewith, John Kerry's attempt to forestall the designation of a brand-new level of travel advisory: Level 5, "seek immediate shelter."

And suddenly my dad's answering the phone, bringing an abrupt end to the beeping of the truck on the line, and saying whatever the Persian equivalent is of hello, his voice much older than I thought it would be. I realize that I'm unprepared to speak to him, that I'm in fact mute, and that until a few seconds ago everything was theory from thousands of miles away. All the men from central casting are gone now, leaving me to stare into the emptiness of the twenty-four-hour daylight of Imam Khomeini International Airport. Imam Khomeini being one reason, even in death, why our children and grandchildren might not have the future they deserve. The CIA being the other reason.

"Hey, Dad," I say. I say it with so much self-assurance and nonchalance that I almost believe it myself. I can hear the easygoing Upstate flowing out of my mouth, American accent times two.

It's been a long time since someone has said *hey* to my dad. It's been a long time since someone has said *Dad* to my dad. He's speaking Persian back, an uninterrupted sequence of dashes and dots, which, spoken aloud in real time, shares none of the hand-drawn lyricism of the signs surrounding me. He's the one who sounds anxious and awkward. Then there's a pause, and I'm not sure if this is where I'm supposed to continue trying to make myself known or if the line has gone dead. I fear that this phone call is a good indication that what awaits my dad and me will be a reunion of discomfort, miscommunication, and regret. Lovely seeing you once again, we will say, with woodenness and obligation, shaking hands when we part.

But my dad is saying, "Danny?" He has flicked the switch into English, groping for understanding. "Danny, is this you?" He's chosen not to use my Persian name, which is disconcerting for me, because if not here, then where? If not him, then who? In English his voice is soft and solicitous, dare I say paternal, but his accent is extra-thick and he seems to be adding syllables to single-syllable words, he's going up at the end of sentences when he should be going down. I have to concentrate, I have to press the phone to my ear, and I can't help but wonder if my dad was indeed the author of that florid email he'd sent about the natural splendors of Iran, or if he'd copied-and-pasted it straight off of a travel blog.

"Yes, it's me," I say, name unstated and nonchalance maintained. We're just catching up here, loosey-goosey, enacting the inverse of acute anxiety.

"Danny, where are you?" he says.

I tell him where I am. He is relieved to hear where I am. He makes it sound as if there was a chance I wouldn't have arrived, or that I wouldn't have been allowed in, or that I wouldn't be allowed to make a phone call; this is, after all, Level 4. He wants to know how the flight was. The flight was terrible, I want to say. "The flight was great," I say, because I'm easygoing from Upstate. What I'm really hoping is that he's on his way to pick me up, to surprise me with some hospitality at the airport, but there's no way of asking about this without seeming entitled. If I was speaking to Chip, I'd say, Hey, Chip, are you coming to pick me up at the airport? But this isn't Chip, and my dad is telling me to take a taxi to the hotel. "Don't get ripped off by the driver," he tells me. He sounds paternal again. Or maybe he's just paranoid. I'm impressed that he's used the colloquialism *ripped off*. "We'll have lunch tomorrow," he says. "Does that sound like a plan?"

"That sounds like a plan," I say. He wants to know if I have any of my authority papers with me. What authority papers is he talking about? "Any authority papers," he repeats. Apparently this is how you talk about passports and visas when you're on the phone and the mullahs might be listening.

"Yes, I've brought them," I say.

"Where are they?" he says.

"They are here," I say. "They are in my pocket."

"What are they?" he says.

"*What* are they?" I ask. *They* are my visa and passport and driver's license. What else would they be? Have I forgotten to bring something essential?

Finally, I realize that what he's asking me is if I have any food allergies.

I don't know about the rest of the country, but Tehran is slate-gray in the spring. The gray goes with the beige of the buildings. The beige goes with the black of the head-scarves. The only color is the yellow of the taxi I'm sitting inside, speeding through the city, the cabbie flouting the rules of the road, along with the truck drivers, the bus drivers, and the motorcyclists who aren't wearing helmets. Everyone's honking, everyone's in a hurry, everything looks hardscrabble, but every city can appear hardscrabble when it's overcast and you're coming in from the airport on little sleep. If it weren't for the women with the headscarves and those snowcapped mountains off in the distance, the ones my dad referenced when he'd referenced beauty, I could be driving down the Grand Central Parkway right now. When I'm not staring through the window, I'm staring at the back of the cabbie's head, beige cap on black hair. He knows enough English to know that I need to get to the hotel. He's about my age, give or take, probably having to drive a taxi for a living because it's the only way he can make ends meet under the economic sanctions—the economic sanctions being one more reason why our children and grandchildren aren't going to have the future they deserve. He'd tried to help me with my luggage curbside, but I didn't want to come across as entitled, and so I did it myself, a big jet-lagged smile on my face. I'm sure he can tell I'm American without me even opening my mouth, unless he's guessing Italian or Greek. Or maybe he can see straight through the facade to what's really going on behind Danny McDade. It's not my fault, I want to tell him, meaning the economic sanctions and whatever else might be my fault. In addition to the exhaustion and befuddlement, I'm operating with guilt and shame, my own and my country's, the latter about a century in the making. In that alternate reality of mine, the one where WASP mom moved to Iran, circa 1983, tail end of the Cultural Revolution, I can picture in my jet-lagged state how *I'd* be the thirty-five-year-old cabdriver in this present-day scenario, Danush Jamshid from Hormozgan Province, doing what I can to make ends meet in a country that has an oil embargo, banking restrictions, and frozen assets. I'd be driving from the airport at top speed, flouting the rules of the road because I have nothing to lose, swerving to avoid the pedestrians who are crossing in the middle of the street since they have nothing to lose, either.

In my spare time, I'd be selling knockoff SIM cards, trying to make extra money on the side so I can save enough to get to America, never mind that there's a Muslim ban, never mind that I'm filled with envy and disdain for the American sitting in the backseat of my taxi who was too petrified to even let me help him with his luggage. I'd be dreaming of Amazon and Walmart and women without headscarves, hoping I'd have the chance one day to study engineering at Long Island University, because I've heard it's a good school, and it's also my sole chance at circumventing global bureaucracy. And lo and behold, in this alternate reality of mine, Danush Jamshid would somehow have his visa application approved—I don't know how, this is all flight of fancy anyway—but when he arrives in America that's where the fancy ends for good and the truth takes over, where he finds he still needs to drive a taxi to make ends meet, nights and weekends, going up and down the Grand Central Parkway in big bad New York City, because that's what an immigrant from a Level 4 country does when he can't put his engineering degree to use and he's overstayed his visa. He'll be picking up people at the airport who'll stare at the back of his head, wondering how much English he speaks.

By the time the cabdriver pulls up to my hotel, I would have been more than happy if he'd rip me off. I give him seventy-five thousand tomans, which sounds like more than it is. I want to say something meaningful, something about how he should never give up on the dream, brother. He tries to help me with my luggage, but of course that's not going to happen. A moment later, he's disappeared back into traffic, eight lanes where there should be six, leaving me standing on the sidewalk staring up at my hotel that says HOTEL in English, which I find comforting. It's a building that's obviously been designed with the Western conception of the Orient, borderline kitsch to put people like me at ease, with its purple paisley exterior to set it apart from the municipal gray. On top of the portico is a statue of an elderly man in repose, sitting cross-legged and wearing a turban. He looks like a character from Disney, the flip side of fundamentalism, olde worlde and defanged, just returned from having bartered spices on the Silk Road, when times were simpler, before there were centrifuges and enriched uranium. Come inside the hotel, he seems to be saying in mildly accented English, we will neither loathe nor envy you, we are only delighted that you are here to spend some money. He's either a stereotype or the source material for what becomes a stereotype, and I'm not well versed enough to know the difference. Framing the hotel entrance are two life-sized sculptures of white stallions, rearing with excitement, so that when I wheel my luggage past I can feel like a conquering hero, which I also find comforting. Inside the lobby, there are Persian ornamental vases, six feet tall, and there are Persian rugs on the Persian floors, and there's an aquarium with Persian fish swimming in a loop. The hotel staff is friendly, bilingual, and all male, and they appear, each and every one of them, to exhibit no signs of monetary distress or international disdain. My dad is picking up the tab for this gaudy hotel, six days and five nights. He'd offered. I'd said no. He'd said it was the least he could do. I was adamant. He was adamant. We went back and forth like this for a while, until I realized he was right, it *was* the least he could do.

The last time I saw my dad was in Buffalo, New York, of all places, speaking of hardscrabble. I was almost twenty years old then, and I'd taken the train one winter morning to meet him, seven hours door-to-door from the suburbs of Upstate, with my mom and Chip seeing me off on the platform. They were smiling and waving, putting on happy faces. "Have fun," Chip called, but I could see the forlorn glimmer in his eyes. Then I spent the next seven hours watching the state of New York pass by my train window, mountains, lakes, rivers, thinking about trying to have fun. When I arrived it was early afternoon, and whatever the temperature had been in Upstate, it was half that in Buffalo, the midday wind blowing hard across the platform, and there was my dad waiting for me under the exit sign, smiling and waving, showing Persian hospitality, and dressed in sandals and socks. I was confused by this, the sandals and socks, and the confusion embarrassed me, and the embarrassment overwhelmed any other emotion I might have had the chance to feel. Amid the crowd of departing train travelers, my dad had stood out as conspicuously foreign, and this, as I already knew, was something one sublimated as best one could. I'd worn a jacket and slacks for the occasion, the all-American wardrobe bought at Walmart, because my mom and Chip had insisted I look presentable when seeing my dad after fifteen years. The first thing he did, in lieu of a hug, was make a big production out of comparing the height of our shoulders to see if I'd outgrown him yet at the age of twenty. As far as icebreakers went, it was a good one, and we'd stood there on the train platform, negative windchill, sandals and socks, acting as if we were buddies from way back, pressing our shoulders together. When my dad saw that I was indeed an inch taller, he was ecstatic. "You've surpassed me!" he said. His accent was thick and his syntax perfect and his phrase was infused with double meaning. He was acting casual and upbeat. He was also asserting that, regardless of fifteen years of separation, biology could not be expunged.

Then we walked. I was cold and he was not. I somehow knew that to tell my dad I was cold would be to acknowledge that I was an American, fragile, privileged, cloistered, all true and, in this context, unbecoming. There was an Iranian restaurant he was keen on taking me to for lunch, a very special restaurant that would have *doogh*, the best yogurt drink I'd ever had. "*Doogh*," he said, as if I would of course understand what *doogh* was and why we needed to walk so far to have a glass. I had never heard of this yogurt drink before. I had never heard that yogurt was something one could drink. "*Doogh*," my dad kept saying. I wasn't sure if he was saying "do," "dug," or "dough." I wasn't sure if I should call him *Dad* and he wasn't sure if he should call me *Danush*, so we wisely avoided the conundrum by calling each other nothing. I asked him if we might pass Niagara Falls on the way to the restaurant, but he said no, Niagara Falls was on the other side. "We'll do it next time," he said. Sure, he'd been bouncing from city to city for the last fifteen years, engineering job to engineering job, West Coast, Florida, Texas, not to mention Queens, but that was the past, and now, at the age of fifty, he was stable, he was putting down roots, he was here to stay in Buffalo, seven hours away by train.

Once my embarrassment had dissipated, curiosity began to take over. I was strolling with a stranger who resembled me slightly, eyes, nose, skin—although mine ten shades lighter, thanks to the woman in this equation. And yet my dad was the one who had remained single after all these years. For what reason, I did not know. There was a lot I did not know.

"Aren't your feet cold?" I asked him.

"American winters," he said, "are nothing like Iranian

winters." He showed me his fingers. His fingers were permanently swollen. "From the Iranian winters," he said. "When I owned no gloves."

Because of the cold, there was hardly anyone else on the street. The emptiness made the city look more desolate than it probably already was. Every so often we would pass an American flag in front of a store or house, flapping innocuously, and it occurred to me that out of all the thousands of American flags I'd seen in my life, including my family's on the Fourth, I had never once been in the presence of someone for whom the flag might one day be flown *against*. But my dad did not seem to notice the flags. What he did notice were the big changes happening in the city, "revitalization," he said, mispronouncing it *revitatalization*, including something new and exciting with the Buffalo Skyway, on the other side that he'd show me next time, that he might have a chance to help design if things shook out the way he hoped. I was impressed that he'd use the colloquialism *shook out*.

When we finally got to the restaurant, the restaurant was closed until dinnertime. We gazed through the window at chairs on tables, as if the chef might come out of the kitchen and make an exception for us. Then we walked on. My dad knew of another restaurant that had this very special yogurt drink, *doogh*, that would also be the best I'd ever had. My toes were cold in my loafers and my legs were cold in my slacks and a few times I said something to the effect of, "I'm up for anything," meaning that I was freezing and willing to eat anywhere.

Soon we were in the business district. The business district looked as if it were going out of business. This time the restaurant was open but my dad stared with displeasure at the menu posted in the window.

"Looks good," I said, upbeat and casual.

No, it was not good. The restaurant was not at all what he remembered the restaurant to be. He wanted to take me to yet another restaurant, just a few blocks away, one that would have decent *doogh*, but not the best. He apologized for this in advance. In a city with a population of minimal Iranians, there seemed to me to be a disproportionate amount of Iranian restaurants from which to choose, and I had the sense that my dad had been planning this lunch for a very long time, and the moment was now here, and the moment was all wrong.

The restaurant we settled on was some sort of Persian fusion, nonspecific, all-inclusive, arabesques on the walls, world music playing, college-student waitstaff. I could tell my dad was disappointed and resigned. The *doogh* here was so-so, he said again, and he ordered it anyway. He said that the *ghormeh sabzi* was average, the *khoresh gheymeh* was okay, the *bademjan* was probably good, because how can you screw up *badmejan*? I made a show of looking over the menu and murmuring interest and assent. When the *doogh* arrived, my dad let his sit on the table untouched, as if in protest, a tall glass of pure white liquid with a straw sticking out of it. I sipped mine cautiously, my American palate unaccustomed to exploration and uncertainty, and then something must have clicked inside of me, deep down on that latent genetic level that's apparently always lying in wait, because I instantly recognized it as one of the most delicious things I'd ever tasted, half yogurt, half salt, hint of mint. I sipped and then I gulped, and then it was gone, and I was sucking through the straw, trying to vacuum up the bottom of the glass. Had I been having lunch with Chip, I would have suggested we order another one right away. Instead, I said nothing, because I didn't want to seem entitled.

Now that the central dilemma of finding a restaurant had been resolved, and my dad and I were finally sitting face-to-face, his face somewhat similar to my face, it was clear that the only thing for us to do was engage in small talk, prolonged and small, beginning with the arabesques hanging on the walls. This arabesque represents this, my dad said, that arabesque represents that. He was in docent mode, guiding me through the gallery of antiquities in his sandals and socks. I murmured interest and assent. I asked follow-up questions. I waited for the waiter. By the way, my dad said, had he mentioned that the *badmejan* in this restaurant was good? Yes, he had mentioned that. But thank you for mentioning that again. I will order that because you have now mentioned that. I spoke the way I was dressed, jacket and slacks for maximum courtesy and inoffensiveness. I leaned in close so I could hear his every word, my hands folded, my elbows off the table, the small talk made more self-conscious by my dad's accent and the world music being piped in and the laughter emanating from the other tables, especially the one right next to us, where a group of college students, about my age, ate from a dozen different plates of Persian fusion food. They were full-on Americans, no question, just dropping in for some culture on a cold winter's day, but I was sure they knew more about what they were eating than I ever would.

I kept expecting that the small talk with my dad would soon be supplanted with the substantial talk, the talk about what life had been like for me these last fifteen years, about what life had been like after he'd left us, Mom and me in our apartment in outer Queens, across from the nail salon, Nails Something Something. But the small talk continued unabated. There had been buildup and now there was anticlimax. I was the adopted child who, upon finally meeting his birth parent, marvels at the shared biology, but aside from that, so what?

"Do you remember," my dad suddenly asked me, "the time we drove to Long Island for the weekend?" He was telling me about a time when we'd taken a drive one Sunday afternoon, impromptu, the three of us, early summer in the Buick LeSabre, windows rolled down, final destination Mineola, but then we'd changed our minds at the last minute, and we'd continued on to Shelter Island, an additional two hours away. He gazed at me through the recollection.

I racked my brain for the memory. "No," I said, "I don't remember that."

"Do you remember," he went on, "the time we drove to New Jersey for the weekend?" According to him, the same sequence of events had transpired: the three of us, Sunday afternoon, early summer in the long-ago-discontinued Buick LeSabre, final destination the Palisades, but altered at the last minute.

"That sounds like fun," I said.

I could see him searching through the database in his head, searching, searching, and coming up empty because, after all, there were only a handful of memories to choose from, and now the small talk was replaced by silence, prolonged and telling, my dad and I avoiding eye contact, while the table of my American peers stuffed their faces with plates of *ghormeh sabzi*. I thought perhaps I should try to offer my own reminiscences from the past, but all I had were bits and pieces of non-narrative. Do you remember the time you were sitting on the blue couch? Do you remember the time you put the hard-boiled egg on my plate?

After a while, my dad asked me if I happened to remember the time we went to Coney Island. There had been no

Buick LeSabre for this outing, only the subway, the three of us on the F train coming in from Queens, forty stops end-to-end. He was looking at me from across the table with an almost pleading look, a please-tell-me-you-remember-this look, how is it possible that you don't remember this? In his mind it must have felt like this had taken place just last week, the three of us oceanside, me, Mom, and Dad, walking on the boardwalk to buy frozen ice from a vendor, and then my dad taking me on the merry-go-round. How can you not remember the merry-go-round? When I was done with the merry-go-round we went into the water, and the waves were gentle, and I had water wings and an inflatable dolphin that he'd bought for me right after he'd bought me the frozen ice from the vendor. He said he'd shown me how to float on my back, and how to kick my legs, and we played some game with the inflatable dolphin, and when we were done with the water he took me back on the merry-go-round again.

"Do you remember that?" he asked.

"Yes," I said, "I remember that."

———

As it turns out, Tehran is beautiful in the spring. The temperature is just right, and there's a gentle breeze blowing, and the snowcapped mountains loom so large and look so close. My dad lives about a mile from the hotel if you walk straight down the main thoroughfare, and then turn right, and left, and right again, which I do, thanks to the friendly staff at the hotel who circled points A, B, and C on my map, showing patience with the American. I'm blinking in the sunlight, which seems extra-bright because of day two of jet lag—it's noon when it should be night—and once again I'm dressed in jacket and slacks for the occasion, because I want to look presentable when seeing my dad for the first time in fifteen years, but also because I thought I'd read somewhere that it's not acceptable for men in Iran to wear short sleeves in public. Apparently I'd been wrong about that, as I'd been wrong about many things, including the grimness, the hopelessness, the ruthlessness that I was so sure I'd been able to perceive blurring past the window of my taxi. Whereas yesterday there'd only been gray, beige, and black, today there's color everywhere, pastels and primaries, even the women's headscarves are in color. In that alternate reality of mine, Danush Jamshid would be taking an afternoon break from selling his knockoff SIM cards so that he could meet his dad for lunch, just catching up, he'd be driving his motorcycle at top speed down the main thoroughfare, no helmet needed. Instead, I'm Danny McDade, walking among the people of Level 4, pretending as if I'm one of them, the diaspora having come full circle. I don't need to speak the language to know that something like happiness can still exist in a nation that has an oil embargo, banking restrictions, and frozen assets. Every few blocks I pass a mural in vivid detail and vibrant color, meticulously painted, five, six, seven stories high, of rainbows, angels, doves, optimism. Later, I will ask my dad to explain the symbolism to me and he will say that these are not symbols but commemoration of the Iran-Iraq War in which a million died.

Unlike the hotel, my dad's apartment building has not been designed with the Western conception of the Orient. It's a plain, no-nonsense structure, closer to Queens than the Orient. There might as well be a nail salon across the street. The stairwell is constructed out of pale concrete, making it seem as if the entire building will crumble at the first tremor, and it's while walking up this stairwell, my loafers making hollow sounds, that I suddenly think that I should have brought something for lunch, just a little box of something to show American hospitality and that I've been raised right. "Here's a little box of something that I picked up," I'd say. But it's too late now, and I'm standing in front of my dad's door, staring at a nameplate handwritten in Persian, which I'm assuming says *Jamshid*. It's as beautiful as any of the signs I've seen, this one simple word, and I realize that it's the first time I've witnessed my dad's handwriting, with its calligraphic expertise, its dashes and dots, reading right to left. Then again, it might be the landlord's handwriting.

My dad opens the door, as if he's heard my footsteps in the stairwell, and he hugs me, right there in the doorway, fifteen years gone by like that. He's not worrying about my height or about icebreakers. I can feel his full weight leaning into me. "How have you been?" he says. He's saying it into my shoulder. I don't know if he's asking me how I've been since arriving in Iran, or how I've been for the last fifteen years.

He's been aging, that's how *he's* been. He has gray in his bushy eyebrows and he's stooping a bit. I can still see my resemblance in him, at least I think I can, the inescapable biology, the nose, skin, etc. I wonder if I'll start to stoop when I'm sixty-five, if that's what I have to look forward to. Meanwhile, he's ushering me into his apartment. If he's anxious about anything, he doesn't seem it. His apartment is decorated like the hotel lobby, paisley on the walls, Persian rugs on the floor, but the place is sparse and has the quality of a bachelor pad. It feels as if it's been recently cleaned and before that had not been cleaned in a year. If I were to open a dresser drawer I'd find a bag of potato chips. The living room table has been laid out with bowls of pomegranates, apricots, and pistachios: the source material for what becomes Hollywood cliché. "This is just to get us started," my dad says. He sounds excited. He's been waiting for this moment, and now the moment has arrived, and he's going to make sure the moment is perfect.

I don't drink tea, but I say I do, and he pours me a cup from a giant bronze samovar that looks ancient and inoperable. If the samovar makes the tea taste better than a teapot,

I can't tell. Then we sit cross-legged on the paisley cushions on the Persian rug, drinking tea and eating pomegranates, apricots, and pistachios, trying to catch up. "Have you ever had pomegranates before?" my dad asks. "Yes, I have," I say. "These are the best pomegranates," he says. I'm trying not to get red juice all over my mouth. I'm trying not to get pistachios in my teeth. I'm trying to listen and not make mistakes. I'm in polite mode. I'm thirty-five years old and I'm not accustomed to sitting cross-legged on the floor.

He's retired now from engineering. He's all finished with what his LIU education gave him. He points to his college diploma hanging on the wall. He's proud of that college diploma in its ready-made frame. It looks like a prop that he's hung for the occasion, and when I leave, he'll take it down. He's done moving from city to city. He's stable. He's here to stay in Tehran, fourteen hours away by plane.

Halfway through catching up I spill some of the tea on the Persian rug and panic. It looks like raindrops before the hard rain comes. "Sorry about that!" I say, but my dad shrugs. In a bachelor pad you don't care about spilled tea. The drops sit between us, slowly drying, while my dad asks me if I remember how we had to walk through Buffalo trying to find lunch at a Persian restaurant. "Of course I do," I say. He asks me if I remember the *doogh* I drank. "The so-so *doogh*," he says. I ask him if he remembers that he'd worn sandals and socks. Yes, he remembers that. He's laughing, and so am I. Here's the memory that we've managed to create, the funny story about a cold afternoon in Buffalo. Now I've got five days left on a thirty-day visa and my dad is telling me that he has big, big plans for us. First we're going to go to a museum to see the national treasures. Then we're going to eat at a real Persian restaurant. Then we're going to take an excursion to the mountains. He pulls the paisley drape back so I can see the top of the snowcapped mountains from his window. "Just an afternoon trip," he says, because the mountains are deceptively close. I'm sure that when the Americans have grown tired of waiting around for the sanctions to bring about regime change, forty years and counting, they won't invade from the sea, but will instead choose to come over those mountains.

"You'll see," my dad tells me, "we're going to experience it all."

ACKNOWLEDGMENTS

As always, this book could not have been written without my wife, Karen Mainenti, and my therapist, Steven Kuchuck.

I am indebted to my agent, Zoë Pagnamenta, and to Alison Lewis and Jess Hoare at the Zoë Pagnamenta Agency, and to my editor Matt Weiland, who years ago plucked me from obscurity while I was working for Martha Stewart. My gratitude also to Cressida Leyshon, Deborah Treisman, David Remnick, Hilton Als, Ian Parker, Peter Carey, Tom Sleigh, Jennifer Raab, Andy Polsky, Joanna Yas, Jerome Murphy, Deborah Landau, Anya Backlund, Alison Granucci, Victor LaValle, Dani Shapiro, Michael Maren, Hannah Tinti,

Bryan Charles, Scott Smith, Andrew Fishman, Jeff Golick, Jeff Adler, and Thomas Beller, who years ago plucked me from obscurity on the basketball court. As well as to the New York Foundation for the Arts, Blue Flower Arts, Hunter College, Columbia University, and New York University, where several of these stories were written sitting in a cubicle in the basement of Bobst Library.